COPPER

TEAGAN
BROOKS

COPPER

BLACKWINGS MC - DEVIL SPRINGS - BOOK ONE

TEAGAN BROOKS

CONTENTS

To my Tiny.
Everything I do is for you.
I love you.

1

COPPER

I pulled up to Badger's cabin several hours later than planned. I was supposed to arrive earlier in the day, but club business held me up. Luckily, it wasn't anything my VP, and brother by blood, couldn't handle, so I took off as soon as I had the chance.

It didn't happen often, but every once in a while, I needed to get away and spend a few days by myself. Luckily, the VP of the Croftridge Blackwings, Badger, had a remote cabin close by and was willing to let me use it whenever I wanted, as long as it wasn't being used by him or one of the other brothers.

The cabin itself was more extravagant than

necessary for me, but beggars couldn't be choosers and all. The two-story monstrosity sat in a clearing near the top of Meadow Ridge Mountain, and it was as remote as you could get and still have some of modern society's conveniences, like power and spotty cell phone service. The views were breathtaking, and the quiet was priceless. I could already feel the tension leaving my body as soon as I climbed off my bike.

After putting my things away and showering to wash the road from my body, I managed to round up something to eat. I planned on stopping at the grocery store at the bottom of the mountain, but I didn't have enough time before it got dark. The road to the cabin wasn't paved, and it was dangerously narrow in a few spots. The single headlight on my bike didn't provide enough illumination for me to risk it.

After dinner, I went out to the back deck to have a beer. As I sat gazing at the horizon watching the sun descend behind the trees, I wondered where my life was going. From the outside looking in, most would think I was on top of the world. I wasn't overly wealthy, but I lived comfortably. I was the president of a local chapter of a well-known motorcycle club. And there were plenty of women around who were willing to keep my bed warm. So, why did it feel like something was missing?

Sighing, I closed my eyes and tried to relax. The answers to my problems wouldn't come when I was actively searching for them; they never did. My moments of clarity arrived at the least expected—and usually the most inconvenient—times. As my stress melted away, I started to drift off into a light sleep.

A shrill scream piercing the night air had me jumping to my feet and grabbing my gun before my conscious mind was fully awake. I knew better than to fall asleep outside at dusk. There were plenty of predatory animals in the area, including cougars and bears. And it sounded like a cougar was close by. I never understood why they didn't roar like the other big cats. Instead, they sounded more like a woman screaming.

I quickly turned on the tactical light mounted on my gun and scanned the surrounding trees, hoping like hell I didn't see any glowing eyes. I had no desire to kill the animal, but I would if it came down to it or me. Typically, they would run away from humans, but wild animals were just that, wild, and I wasn't taking any chances.

Slowly backing up toward the cabin, I continued to sweep the landscape with my light. I was almost to the door when I heard another scream. And it was clearly human.

Flinging the back door open, I grabbed the rifle Badger kept in the coat closet and holstered my gun. I was already walking in the direction I thought the scream came from when I heard it again. This time it sounded more like a woman crying. As I got closer, I could hear snarling and growling from more than one animal. I raised the rifle and placed my finger on the trigger as I moved deeper into the forest until I came upon one of the last things I ever expected to see.

A visibly terrified woman was precariously perched on top of a large boulder while two wild boars were on the ground snarling and desperately trying to get to her. Without hesitation, I aimed and fired twice, in quick succession, striking each boar in the head and permanently silencing them. However, I could still hear the woman screaming, even with my ears ringing from the two shots.

I held my hands up in front of me as I slowly started to approach her. Her eyes widened in fear before darting wildly around the area. I knew what she was doing— looking for an escape.

As predicted, seconds later, she leaped from the boulder and took off in a full sprint deeper into the trees. What the hell? Did she not realize the boars came from the forest and likely had friends in the area? Not to mention the more ferocious predators she could encounter.

My extensive training kicked in, and I reacted on pure instinct. I dropped the rifle and went after her. The woman was fast, I'd give her that, but she wasn't as fast as me. I quickly caught up with her and realized the only way to catch her was to take her down. My hand snagged her shirt, and I pulled her to me. With my arms wrapped around her torso, I turned so that my body would hit the ground first instead of hers. As soon as we landed, I quickly reversed our positions and hovered over her.

Her eyes were filled with fear and, unexpectedly, anger. What did she have to be angry about? I just saved her from a pair of wild beasts. She struggled against me, and I started to lose my patience. "Calm down, woman. I'm not going to hurt you," I barked, harsher than I intended, but whatever.

She froze at my words but remained silent. "Care to tell me just what in the hell you're doing out here?"

She didn't answer me; just continued to stare at me with a stunned look on her face.

"Answer me. This is private property, and you're trespassing."

She remained silent for a few more beats before she started to struggle again.

Fuck that!

I rose to my feet, pulling her up with me. Before she could move, I bent and hoisted her over my shoulder. If she didn't want to talk outside, maybe she would inside. We didn't need to be out in the open anyway. It wouldn't be long before other animals in the area smelled the boars' blood and came for a snack.

She wiggled and squirmed, trying to free herself, while I walked back to retrieve the rifle before continuing on to the cabin. I had one arm clamped tightly over her thighs, but the feisty little woman was beating the hell out of my back with her fists.

When we reached the cabin's back deck, enough was enough. With my free hand, I gave her a nice hard slap on her ass, hoping to startle her out of her actions.

She froze for half a second before she started wailing on my back again. If she was going to hit me, I would return the favor. The stubborn woman wouldn't quit. So, I smacked her ass two more times before I stepped inside and propped the rifle against the wall by the back door.

That's when she chose to sink her teeth into the flesh right beneath my shoulder blade, and that was the equivalent of declaring war in my book. I grabbed a roll of duct tape from Badger's junk drawer and tossed her onto the couch. Within seconds, I had her arms and legs secured. I knew she wouldn't stay put willingly, but she had some questions to answer before I let her leave and restraining her seemed like the easiest way to go about it. First and foremost, she was going to tell me who she was and what she was doing on Badger's property.

I considered carrying her upstairs to one of the bedrooms but thought better of it. She was likely scared out of her mind as it was. I heaved in a breath and tried to gather some patience and understanding. I knew I came off harsher than I usually intended, and I was trying to tamp that down before I started questioning her, if she would only stop screaming.

"Enough!" I roared. "If you don't stop that screaming right this fucking second, I'll cover your mouth with tape and lock you in one of the bedrooms until I feel like trying to deal with you again, which will likely damn well be tomorrow."

Silence. Blessed, wonderful silence. And tears. Fuck me. I hated it when women cried. It was a weakness I had yet to overcome.

I exhaled slowly and softened my voice. "Like I said, I'm not going to hurt you. You don't need to be scared of me."

She narrowed her eyes and said, "Says the man who hit me, restrained me with tape, and threatened to lock me in a bedroom. Tell me, when do the whips and chains appear?"

"They won't if you lose the attitude and start answering my questions," I said flatly.

"You haven't asked any questions."

"Yes, I did. Outside. Never mind. I'm not arguing with you. What were you doing traipsing around on private property?"

"I wasn't traipsing around. I was out hiking, and I got lost. Then, I walked up on those feral pigs, and they started chasing me. When I saw the boulder, I figured it was my best chance to get away from them," she said, not once meeting my eyes during her explanation.

"You go hiking without a pack often?" I asked, not believing her bullshit for one second.

She blinked and visibly swallowed. "I dropped it so I could run faster."

I nodded and rubbed my chin with my thumb and forefinger. "You aren't wearing the proper attire for hiking," I observed as I scanned her from head to toe. That's when I saw it. Blood, seeping from underneath her calf. "What happened to your leg?"

She suddenly grimaced, as if she had forgotten about it until I mentioned it. "I think one of them got my leg when I was climbing up the rock."

"Oh, hell. Let me see how bad it is," I said and approached her without waiting for permission. She grunted when I rolled her over but didn't give any other kind of protest.

Gently pulling the torn denim apart, I sucked

in a sharp breath when I saw the gaping wound. "Shit, it looks like one gored your calf with its tusk. We need to get you to the hospital."

She rolled herself to her back and let out a pained groan before insisting, "No! No hospital."

I arched a brow and waited for more. When she didn't offer any further explanation, I asked, "Why?"

"Just, please, no doctor, no hospital," she begged, her eyes wild with panic.

I nodded. "Okay, no doctor, but that wound needs to be cleaned and stitched. It's going to hurt like a bitch with no anesthetic. I got some whiskey in the kitchen that might take the edge off," I offered.

"I'll take the whiskey," she said with no hesitation.

"Be right back," I said with a small smile.

I walked to the far side of the kitchen and placed a call to Splint. He was a member of my club, but he worked as a paramedic and had quite a bit of medical training from his days in the military. "Brother, I need you to bring your kit up to Badger's cabin. I got a girl up here that got gored by a boar on her calf. It's pretty nasty, and she's refusing to go to the hospital."

"Sure thing, Prez. Heading out now," he said.

"And, Splint, keep this shit to yourself."

He chuckled. "Yes, Prez."

When I poured the glass of whiskey, I also mixed in a crushed sleeping pill. It wasn't ideal, but refusing to go to the hospital left limited options. At least this way, she would wake with a cleaned and stitched wound without having to suffer through the pain.

Carrying the homemade anesthetic in one hand and a beer for myself in the other, I returned to the living room to find her struggling to remove the tape from her wrists. I shook my head and sighed in exasperation. "I was considering removing the tape, but clearly, it's too soon. I'm going to help you sit up so you can drink this down," I said and held up the glass of whiskey.

She nodded and eyed me warily. I reached under her arms and hoisted her to a sitting position, being careful to keep her leg from dragging along the couch's textured fabric. "Here you go," I said and held the glass of whiskey to her lips. She tentatively took a sip and hissed at the burn when she swallowed.

"It tastes funny," she said.

"It's an aged whiskey, so it has a stronger taste than your run-of-the-mill whiskeys. Can have a bit of an aftertaste, too, at least for the first few sips," I told her, like I was some kind of whiskey connoisseur. I was just spouting off random bullshit so she would drink it and pass out.

She nodded and continued to drink. Good. With any luck, she would be out cold by the time Splint arrived to take care of her leg. I studied her while she sipped from the glass. She was incredibly beautiful, yet somehow, she seemed familiar, though I couldn't place her. She had long, golden blonde hair and sparkling blue eyes. Her lips were full and enticing, perfect for...I shook my head, refusing to let my mind go there. Luckily, she finished the drink within a few moments, and I returned to the kitchen to wait for Splint.

When Splint arrived, the woman was sound asleep on the couch. He inspected her wound and suggested we move her to one of the bedrooms.

"She's going to flip when she wakes up, but if that's better for you, let's do it," I said.

Two hours later, Splint came out of her room and found me drinking a beer on the couch. "That was a nasty wound, Prez. She's going to have to take very good care of it and keep a close watch on it for infection. I flushed it out as best I could and gave her an injection of antibiotics, but that might not be enough. Wounds like that almost always get infected."

"If you have more medicine with you, I can give her another dose or two, if you think that's what she needs," I offered.

"Yeah, I do. She'll need an injection every twelve hours for at least three more doses. Then, she can probably switch to pills; one every twelve hours for ten days. Even with the antibiotics, she needs to watch it closely. If it gets infected and isn't taken care of properly, she could easily lose her leg," Splint said while digging through his kit for the antibiotics.

"Thanks, brother. Appreciate you getting here so fast and taking care of her leg for me."

Splint eyed me with a sly grin on his face, "No problem, Prez. You gonna tell me how you ended up with a woman who'd been bitten by a wild boar in your possession?"

"No, I am not, and you're not going to tell anyone else about it either," I snapped.

"Got it, Prez. If you don't need anything else, I'm going to head back to the clubhouse."

"I think we're good. Thanks, Splint. See you in a few days," I said and walked him to the door.

Once he was gone, I dropped my ass onto the couch and wondered what in the hell I was going to do with the woman upstairs.

2

LAYLA

My head was throbbing, and there was a very good chance I was going to throw up. Rolling to my side, I started to get out of bed to go to the bathroom when the excruciating pain in my lower leg had me freezing in place. I took in a few deep breaths and slowly opened my eyes.

Oh, crap. Where in the hell was I? I whipped my head around, causing the throbbing to ramp up to a damn near intolerable level. I quickly realized I wasn't in my room. Well, it wasn't exactly my room, but it had come to feel like it was mine since I had been sleeping there every night for longer than I cared to admit. I tried desperately to remember what happened to me, but I was drawing a blank. Between the pain in my leg and the pulsing in my brain, it was all I could do to make it to the door that hopefully led to a bathroom.

I did my business, washed my face, and rinsed my mouth out with some mouthwash I found under the sink. Unfortunately, after a quick perusal of the medicine cabinet, I didn't find anything to help with the pain.

Tiptoeing back to the bed, I gingerly sat and inspected my leg. My jeans had been cut away at the knee, and my calf was covered in a large bandage. I teetered back and forth on whether or not I should take a peek. Ultimately, I figured if it was hurting as bad as it was, I should have a look and see what was causing the pain since my memory was still failing me.

Carefully, I pulled the tape back from the top corner of the dressing and lifted the gauze away from my skin. The sight of the grotesque wound on my calf had me gasping in horror. A huge gash surrounded by some serious bruising covered the majority of my calf. But what stumped me even more were the professional looking stitches. Well, thank you to whomever, but I needed to get out of wherever I was and back to my safe haven.

I glanced around the room and found two windows on the back wall of the bedroom. Hobbling over, I peeked outside and realized I was in the cabin. What was I doing inside?

What was even more disturbing was that I couldn't recall anything. Obviously, someone found me and brought me inside. But how did they find me and what happened to my leg?

Huffing out a breath in frustration, I mentally chastised myself. I needed to focus on getting out of the cabin as soon as possible because I had clearly been discovered by someone, and not knowing who exactly was troubling me the most. It could be any of the three people looking for me, or it could be an all new hell if my history was anything to go by. It would explain why my head was in a fog. I experienced the exact same feelings the last time I was drugged.

Pushing those thoughts away, I eased open the window and mouthed a silent "thank you" for its smooth and soundless slide. Next, I yanked the sheet from the bed and tied it securely to the headboard. Then, I tied a blanket to the end of the sheet, hoping it would be long enough to reach the ground because I didn't see any other material I could use.

Ignoring the pain in my leg, I climbed through the window and began my descent to the ground below hoping and praying the bed wouldn't move and alert whomever was in the house to my activities. The sun was barely peeking over the horizon, so, hopefully, the cabin's occupant was still asleep, and I could get away scot-free.

As soon as my feet touched the ground, I moved as fast as my leg would allow to the bunker I'd been staying in since I managed to escape not one, not two, but three horrible situations. I was beginning to think I had done something to forever piss off Lady Luck until I stumbled upon an unlocked, unoccupied, and fully stocked bunker behind a large cabin.

Once I was safely inside the bunker, I closed the hatch and didn't come out for two whole days. Those first two nights were horrible. I was terrified of what could possibly be coming for me outside. When I was finally brave enough to leave the bunker, I opened the hatch to find the ground covered in snow. There was no way I could try to hike down the mountain in the snow. The only footwear I had was the pair of flimsy tennis shoes I'd been wearing the day I escaped.

So, I stayed in the bunker and waited for the

snow to melt. And it finally did, several weeks later. I should have known if it was warm enough for me to be out and about it was warm enough for the animals in the area to be out scavenging for food. But the thought never occurred to me, and I only made it a few hundred yards from the cabin when I ran into the boars.

I wanted to curl up into a ball and cry, but I couldn't because I needed to come up with a new game plan. There was no way I would be able to get down the mountain with my leg injury, at least not in one day like I'd originally hoped. My head felt fuzzy, and my leg was killing me. I had no idea what to do, and sheer panic was trying its best to consume me as I ambled around the small space, packing everything I could into a large backpack I found in the bunker.

As I was packing, and panicking, an idea hit me. I didn't have to make it down the mountain in one day. I could hike a little bit at a time and then pitch a tent for the night. It would likely take me a few days of hiking and camping before I reached the small town at the base, but I could do it. Once there, I could find someone to help me.

Feeling slightly better about my situation, I hurried to gather the items I needed so I could get out of there before the man came looking for me. Wait! A man? How did I know it was a man in the cabin? Little flashes of memories were blinking on my mind's horizon but refused to light up completely. It didn't matter. I would remember what happened, or I wouldn't. Either way, I didn't have the time to worry about it. Getting away was priority number one.

Once I finished packing, I tossed my loaded backpack through the hatch, followed by the compact two-person tent I found in a storage closet. Then, I climbed out, picked up my belongings, and made a beeline for the trees.

It was taking every bit of my willpower to keep going despite the pain in my leg. I hadn't even made it a third of a mile when I felt like it would be easier and less painful to cut the damn thing off. Tears began to leak from my eyes, but I gritted my teeth and pushed on. This was no time to be weak. If I wanted to survive, I had to keep going. And keep going is what I did.

3

COPPER

I couldn't decide if I was more pissed off or intrigued by the woman as I watched her descend to the ground using a blanket. It was a move I hadn't expected from her, while at the same time, I wasn't surprised by it either.

I watched her limp toward the back of the property and thought briefly about calling out to her, to tell her to stop, but something in my gut told me to wait. I always followed my gut instinct. It had never led me in the wrong direction.

My jaw dropped as I watched her open the hatch to the bunker and climb inside. How did she get in there? It was a fucking bunker for crying out loud. It was supposed to be secure! On second thought, maybe my open-ended invitation to use Badger's cabin had been rescinded, or maybe my brothers in Croftridge were dealing with a situation I wasn't aware of.

Before I could think better of it, I pulled out my phone and dialed Badger. He would be pissed at the early hour, but it couldn't be helped.

"This better be good, Copper," Badger grumbled into the phone.

"It might be; you tell me. Do you have a woman staying in your bunker at the cabin?" I asked, trying to keep my tone light and casual.

"WHAT?" he yelled, damn near rupturing my eardrum.

"You heard me. I came up to the cabin last night to stay for a few days. Found her just inside the tree line sitting on top of a huge boulder trying to get away from a couple of wild boars. This morning, I watched her sneak out of a window upstairs and run off to the bunker."

"Why was she in the cabin?" he asked.

"Because one of the boars got her leg. She tried to run away after I shot the beasts, but I caught her. I was going to question her, but then I realized she was hurt. Called Splint to come and sew up her leg. She didn't want to go to the hospital, so I crushed up a sleeping pill and put it in a glass of whiskey for her. She was out within ten minutes and slept until about thirty minutes ago," I explained.

"How the hell did she get into my bunker?" he asked.

"I take it that means she's not a Blackwings' project?"

"Excuse me?"

"She's got damsel in distress written all over her. I thought she might be someone you guys were helping, like with Ember."

"Son of a motherfucking bitch!" he cursed.

"Not following, brother."

"When all that shit went down with Ember, I bet no one thought to lock up the bunker. And I know for a fact no one but me has been up there since then, and I didn't check it," he explained.

"That explains how she got in, but I think we need to know how she found it in the first place, and why she is using it."

"Completely agree. You want me to head up there?"

"Not yet. I'm going to hang back and watch. See what she does. If she tries to take off, I'll follow. No worries, brother. I'll get some answers from her," I said.

"You sure?" he asked.

"Yeah, she's not a threat, but something's going on with her. Honestly, I think it'll be fun to see how this plays out."

He chuckled into the phone, "Only you would. Thanks, Copper. Call if you need me."

"Will do."

I quickly threw together a rudimentary pack in case I needed to track her while keeping my eye on the bunker. As expected, the little sneak tossed two bags out of the hatch before she climbed out. She glanced around one time, picked up the bags, and darted for the trees.

I smiled to myself. Let the hunt begin.

To MY SURPRISE, SHE ONLY HIKED A MILE OR SO from the cabin before she stopped and started setting up a campsite. She worked quickly and efficiently. Once she had her small tent up, she crawled inside and zipped it closed.

I kept my distance, watching her through binoculars. When twenty minutes passed and she still hadn't come out of the tent, I took that as my opportunity to find my own place to camp. As I got myself setup, I couldn't keep my mind off of the mysterious woman. I had so many questions for her when the time came. And it would come. I would make sure of it.

I continued to watch her from afar for the rest of the day. She only came out of the tent to gather some wood and get a small fire started. What was she doing? I fully expected her to keep moving, not pitch a tent a mile from the cabin. By nightfall, it was clear she was staying put for the night.

When early afternoon rolled around the next day and she still hadn't emerged from her tent, I started to worry. I tried to wait her out, but my gut was telling me something was wrong. Giving up on the cat and mouse game, I made my way to her campsite and called out, "Hey! You okay in there?"

Nothing.

I knew she was inside the tent. After spending so many years in the Marines, there was no way she could have gotten past me without me noticing.

"Hello?" I said and lightly shook the tent with my hand.

Nothing.

Chills crept up my spine, and my skin broke out in goosebumps. Something was wrong. I unzipped the tent and crawled half way inside to find her lying on her side with her knees pulled up to her chest, white as a ghost and drenched in sweat. Her eyes were open, staring blankly at me, and she was so still, for a moment, I wondered if I was too late.

"Fuck," I cursed under my breath. "It's okay, sweetheart. I'm going to get you some help."

She blinked, once. I breathed a sigh of relief and took that as her acknowledgment of my words.

I dialed Splint and told him what was going on. "Should I carry her back to the cabin or wait here with her?"

"If you can carry her back to the cabin, that would be best. I'm on my way now. If you're not at the cabin when I get there, I'll call and come to you."

"Thanks. And, Splint, please hurry."

"Will do, Prez."

I carefully scooped her into my arms and started walking back to the cabin. She groaned when I first moved her, but remained silent until we reached the cabin. I, on the other hand, couldn't stop murmuring soothing words to her.

I took her to the same bedroom she was in before and gently placed her on top of the covers. She immediately curled into the fetal position and whimpered. I wanted to help her, but I wasn't sure what I could do for her before Splint arrived.

Luckily, it wasn't an issue as Splint walked through the door less than two minutes later. He took one look at her and cursed. "How many doses of the antibiotics did she get?"

"Just the one, brother. She took off before I had even had a chance to talk to her. I still have all the injections and the pills," I told him.

"All right. I'm going to get an IV started. She needs fluids and antibiotics immediately. Then, I'll take a look at her wound, which I'm sure is infected. It probably needs to be drained and flushed. In all honesty, Prez, if she doesn't show signs of improvement in the next few hours, we're going to need to get her to the hospital," Splint said, all the while gathering his supplies.

"I have no problem taking her to the hospital. She was the one who insisted on no doctors."

He quirked a brow, "Did she say why?"

I shook my head, "No, she didn't. She kind of freaked out at the mention of a doctor."

Splint nodded and quietly worked on the mystery woman. I sat silently while he tended to her. My mind flooded with questions I wouldn't get the answers to any time soon.

My thoughts were interrupted when Splint cleared his throat. "I've done all I can do for now. I need to stay with her and monitor her closely for the next few hours."

When I looked up, a wave of the most revolting smell hit me. "The fuck is that smell?"

Splint nodded to the wad of medical supplies he had in his gloved hands. "The pus I drained from her leg. It wasn't as bad as I was expecting."

"You don't consider *that* bad?" I asked in disbelief.

Splint snorted. "Guess I'm not as sensitive as your delicate ass."

"Oh, fuck off, man. That's rank, and you know it."

"Didn't say it wasn't. Why don't you try to get some sleep while I sit with her? Looks like you could use it."

"You're probably right. Sleeping on the ground in a tiny tent isn't as easy as it once was," I chuckled. "But I'm not sure I could fall asleep even if I wanted to. Something about this whole situation isn't sitting right with me."

"Have you asked Spazz to check her out?"

"No, I don't have anything to give him. I don't even know her name," I said. Sighing, I pushed to my feet, "I'm going to check out the bunker and see if I can find anything that might be helpful." With that, I quietly closed the door on Splint and the woman I decided to refer to as Locks until I found out her name.

A search of the bunker turned up absolutely nothing. There was not one single thing that hadn't already been in the bunker. Next, I headed to her campsite to pack it up as well as search through her belongings. To my surprise, there wasn't anything that didn't come from the bunker at the campsite other than a dirty t-shirt and a pair of worn out tennis shoes.

Once everything was packed, I hiked back to the cabin with more questions instead of answers.

4

LAYLA

I was dying. That was the only plausible explanation for the way I felt. Or maybe I had been hit by a big Mack truck. What happened to me? Every part of my body ached, but my leg was throbbing. On top of that, I needed to pee. How was I going to use the bathroom when I didn't have enough energy to open my eyes?

Energy or not, my eyes shot open when I heard an unfamiliar voice. "Hey there. Looks like you're starting to wake up. Please try to stay calm. You're very sick, and we're doing everything we can to help you get better," a man I was sure I'd never seen before said.

Who was this mind reading man? I blinked

stupidly at him. I had no idea what to say. Given how dry my throat felt, I wasn't even sure I could talk.

"Do you need to use the bathroom?" he asked.

I nodded quickly, eliciting a chuckle from him.

"I need to disconnect your IV first, and then I'll help you get to the bathroom. I'll wait outside if you promise to call me if you get dizzy or feel like you're going to fall, okay?"

"Water," I managed to croak.

"Oh, sorry. Here you go," he said as he held a straw to my lips. "Just a few small swallows to start with."

I did as he instructed and said, "Thank you."

"All right, let's do this." The man's kindness did not match his exterior whatsoever. Yes, I was judging a book by its cover, but everyone in the world was guilty of that at some point or another. Besides, who would expect a muscular, tattooed, bearded man with a variety of piercings to be so gentle?

Once I did my business, complete with an embarrassingly loud sigh of relief, he helped me back to the bed. It was then that I noticed my surroundings. They looked strangely familiar, but I was drawing a blank.

"Where am I?" I asked.

"We'll get to that in a minute. First, I need to change the dressing on your leg. Are you in any pain right now?"

I grimaced, "Yes, I am. My whole body aches, but my leg feels like it has its own heartbeat. What happened to me?"

He gave me a tight smile, "Let me get you something for the pain, and then we'll talk." Before I could object, he left the room.

Moments later, he returned to the room with a syringe in his hand and another man at his side. He pushed the medicine into my IV and started arranging medical supplies on the bed while I pretended not to have an internal freak out. Both men were huge and scary, but the second man did not give off any gentle vibes like the first man.

"I'm going to start on your leg while we talk. I'm Splint, by the way, and this here is Copper," the kind man said. When I remained silent, he continued. "What's your name?"

Without giving it any consideration, I blurted, "Kayla. Kayla West." I was not about to share my real name, though I wondered if I should have chosen a different name to use. But, Kayla was close to Layla, and I knew I would respond to it as if it were my given name.

"Okay, Kayla, do you remember what happened to your leg?"

"No, but it hurts like a motherfucker. Can I watch whatever you're doing?" I asked.

"I wouldn't mind, but you won't be able to see anything since it's on the back of your leg. I can take a picture if you want," he offered.

"I'll pass," I muttered.

He shrugged. "About your leg, for lack of a better description, you were gored by a wild boar. You told us you came across two wild boars while hiking, and they came after you. You said you ran and climbed on top of a large boulder to get away from them. According to your story, one of them got ahold of your leg while you were trying to climb. In my opinion, it looks like one of them got your calf with a lower canine which tore through your skin and some muscle."

As he spoke, the memories slowly came back to me. I remembered running from the boars. I remembered being stuck on top of that boulder for what seemed like hours. I remembered a man shooting the boars, then chasing after me. I looked up and narrowed my eyes. "You!" I spat, pointing an accusatory finger at the other man in the room.

He smirked, "Guess you do remember."

I focused on Splint. "I want him out of here," I demanded.

"Sorry, Kayla. I'm technically his guest. I don't have any right to kick him out," Splint answered.

Fine. If he wouldn't leave, I would. I moved and attempted to get out of bed.

"Whoa. What are you doing?" Splint asked.

"If he won't go, I will," I spat.

"No, you won't," Copper's deep voice rumbled through the room. "You would be dead if it weren't for me. The least you can do is sit your ass down and accept the care you're being given for free."

"Fine, but then I'm out of here. And for the record, I don't like you." Childish? Yes, but it was all I could come up with. The truth was, I wouldn't have been able to get very far on my own; however, there was no way I would admit it.

"You aren't the first, and you won't be the last, Locks," he said with unmistakable arrogance.

"Locks?" I questioned.

"Didn't know your name and needed to call you something other than 'woman.' You reminded me of Goldie Locks, traipsing around in the woods and sneaking into places you don't belong with that mess of blonde hair," he casually explained.

"I was not traipsing!" I screamed.

"Enough," Splint stated. "This isn't good for her. She needs to rest and let her body heal. Getting her so worked up she's trying to leave isn't helping anything."

Copper pinned Splint with a fierce glare, "I'll let you have that one, but don't you speak to me like that again."

"Got it, Pre—Copper," Splint mumbled before he directed his attention to me. "As for you, your leg is infected, severely. Copper found you basically unconscious in a tent in the woods and carried you back to the cabin. I've been giving you IV antibiotics and IV fluids while monitoring you closely. You need to stay put and let me give you the medicines to fight off the infection. If you leave before you've finished the antibiotics, the same thing will happen to you, only you'll be in far worse shape than you are now. You're at risk of losing your leg or dying. Understood?"

I nodded my understanding, even though I was certain he was exaggerating the severity. "How long will I have to stay here?"

"Probably a couple of days. You need several more doses of IV antibiotics before you can switch to pills. Once you switch to the pills, as long as you can change your dressing and promise to finish the antibiotics, you can leave," Splint explained.

I highly doubted I would be free to leave, if the menacing look on Copper's face was anything to go by. I would have to fight that battle when I came to it. In the meantime, it seemed as if there was nothing else I could do except accept the care being provided for me.

Instead of encouraging either one of the two to continue talking, I tilted my head back and closed my eyes. The medicine Splint had given me had taken the edge off the pain in my leg and was perhaps making me drowsy. Before long, I drifted off to sleep, blissfully unaware of my surroundings.

FOR TWO DAYS, I WAS WAITED ON HAND AND FOOT

by Splint. He brought me food, medicine, and assisted me to the bathroom. He didn't talk to me about anything that wasn't directly related to my health. At first, I was thankful for that, but by the end of the second day, I was beyond frustrated. Surely, they had questions for me. I certainly had come up with a list of my own questions for them.

"Knock, knock," Splint called, as he always did before he entered the room. "How are you feeling today?"

"Better than yesterday," I said, which is exactly how I answered him the previous two mornings.

"Great. While you're eating breakfast, I want to go over how to change your dressing. When you're finished, I want to watch you do it to make sure you can handle it when I'm not around."

I nodded and proceeded to inhale my breakfast while he prattled on about clean hands and a sterile field. I wanted to roll my eyes. Seriously, gauze plus tape, not hard.

"Kayla, you have to take this seriously. It's not like putting a bandage on a scraped knee. You have a serious wound in your leg that is very susceptible to infection. You have to do this properly to prevent it from getting infected again," Splint said, sounding irritated with me.

"I am taking this seriously. I heard everything you said to me about thoroughly washing my hands and making sure to not contaminate the sterile field," I said, a little irritated myself.

"Okay, let's see how you do," he said.

Apparently, I could not fumble my way through changing the dressing to his liking, buying me another day trapped in the cabin. At least I was able to move around by myself, and I even managed to take a shower. Unfortunately, that also meant I had to either put my dirty clothes back on or hand wash them in the sink. I opted to wash my underwear and shirt in the sink. I would tackle my jeans another time.

"Knock, knock," Splint called from the other side of the bathroom door.

"You may not come in," I blurted, wrapping the towel tighter around my body.

"You've been in there a long time. I just wanted to make sure you were okay," he said, and I could hear the concern in his tone.

"I'm fine. I'm just waiting for my clothes to dry," I explained.

I heard a whispered curse followed by, "I'll

leave you to it." I thought his reaction was odd, but in all honesty, the whole situation was odd at best.

When I emerged from the bathroom hours later, wearing dry underwear, dirty jeans that were cut off below the knee on one side, and a slightly damp, albeit clean, shirt, I was utterly shocked to find several bags of clothing on my bed. On top of one of the bags was a note:

Hope these fit.

Sorry, we're men.

Clean clothes didn't occur to us.

It wasn't signed, but I knew it had to be from Splint. Copper hadn't said more than two words, if that, to me since he left the room after our heated discussion.

I looked through the bags and pulled out a pair of yoga pants, a t-shirt, a pair of panties, and a tank top with a built-in shelf bra to wear. The shelf bra would do little to nothing to contain the monsters residing on my chest, but it was better than leaving the girls free to wobble to and fro while I washed and dried the only bra I owned.

As I continued going through the bags, I was beyond delighted to discover one bag containing toiletries—girly toiletries. I was half-tempted to take another shower. Instead, I brushed my teeth, swiped on some deodorant, and drenched my face in moisturizer. When all was said and done, I felt like a new woman. I was also exhausted and decided a nap was in order.

5

COPPER

Splint left to go back to Devil Springs shortly after he returned with numerous bags of clothes and toiletries for Locks. It hadn't occurred to either one of us that she might need clean clothes or other necessities such as a toothbrush. I handed him a wad of cash and told him to go get whatever she needed. When he returned, he went over the instructions for her dressing change with me and informed me she could leave, as far as he was concerned, once she demonstrated changing it properly.

Instead of going to her room and having her change the dressing for me, I was waiting for her to come find me. I knew she would because it was obvious she was anxious to leave. Little did she know, she wasn't going anywhere until she answered all of my questions.

I was outside on the deck drinking a beer when Badger called. "What's up, brother?" I answered.

"Madge, from the diner, called this morning to check in. Said there'd been a lot of activity on my side of the mountain. Everything okay up there?"

I snorted. "Depends on your definition of okay," I said and filled him in on what happened with Kayla since I'd last talked to him.

"What's this girl look like?" he asked.

"She's got long blonde hair that's kinda wavy, blue eyes, average height, tight ass, nice tits, probably around twenty-five years old. Why?"

He cleared his throat, and I suddenly had an uneasy feeling. "Madge said a woman matching that description was reported missing a few weeks ago by the woman who lives on the other side of the mountain, Evelyn Carmichael. Evelyn refused to give the woman's name and only gave a vague description. It all sounded fishy, and the Sheriff didn't know what to make of it. Evelyn was in the hospital when she made the report. Claimed she'd fallen down her front stairs and hit her head, but

Sheriff Simmons said there was evidence of a struggle when he went to make sure her place was locked up. But no one ever saw hide nor hair of the woman."

"So, why don't we call Evelyn and ask her if Kayla is the missing woman?"

"I don't know how to get in touch with her right now. Madge said she'd also broken her hip when she fell and was at some rehab place in the city until she healed," he explained.

"Fuck, you think Kayla did that to Evelyn?" I asked in surprise.

"Not a clue, brother. Did you ask Spazz to check her out?"

"Yeah, after I found out her name. He called yesterday and asked for a picture of her. I was able to get one after she fell asleep last night. Haven't heard back from him yet."

"I'll see if Madge knows how to get in touch with Evelyn. In the meantime, I'd keep an eye on that girl, and don't let her go anywhere until we find out what in the hell is going on."

"Will do. Thanks, Badger."

I leaned back in the chair and sighed. The reason I came up to the cabin in the first place was to have a few days of peace and quiet to clear my head. Instead, those few days had been filled with chaos and drama. I was hoping to be able to send Locks on her way after one more night at the cabin so I could finally enjoy some time alone, but it seemed that was no longer in the cards for me.

My phone rang again, and I answered without looking at the screen, assuming it was Badger. "Prez," Spazz said, "Couldn't find anything solid with the name, but I got a hit on the picture you sent, and I'm not comfortable with where the search is taking me."

After spending some time with Byte from the Croftridge chapter, Spazz rarely had issues hacking into anything. "Explain," I ordered.

"The facial recognition software hit on a federal site, the FBI to be exact. I don't know if I could even get into their site, but just trying could bring a world of trouble to our doorstep."

"Okay, don't go any further with the search. I'll make some calls and see if I can get some answers through other channels. Thanks, Spazz."

"No prob, Prez."

Why in the hell would a picture of Locks hit on a site belonging to the FBI? I knew she was hiding something, but I never would have guessed it was anything worthy of federal attention.

Sighing, I dialed my cousin. "Phoenix, I need your help with something."

"It's about damn time. As much as you've helped me and mine over the last couple of years, I've been waiting on the opportunity to return some of the favors. Whatcha got, man?" Phoenix asked, sounding far too pleased with my request for assistance.

I filled him in on Locks and explained the results of Spazz's search. "Do you think Luke would help us out? I don't want to be accused of aiding and abetting a fugitive if it turns out she is a wanted criminal."

"I'm sure he will. He's still trying to get off of my shit list. Send me her name and the picture."

"Thanks, Phoenix."

"Yep. I'll get back to you in a bit," he said and ended the call.

I went back inside after I finished my beer. In the kitchen, I found Locks rifling through the cabinets. "Looking for something?" I asked.

She jumped and squealed at the sound of my voice. Whirling around, she tried to glare at me through the pained grimace on her face. "Food, asshole. I was looking for something to eat so I can take my medicine."

"Have a seat," I said gruffly. "I'll cook something. I'm hungry, too."

"No, thanks. I'll just go back upstairs until you're finished," she huffed.

"Kayla, sit," I ordered.

Her eyes widened in fear, and she quietly dropped her ass onto a barstool. A part of me, a small part, felt bad for scaring her. Another part of me thought she might be a criminal trying to get anything and everything she could from me.

As I started preparing something for dinner, I decided it was well past time for the two of us to have a discussion. Splint mentioned trying a different approach to get her to talk since barking questions and demanding answers hadn't been working. It couldn't hurt to try his method. If it didn't prove to be fruitful, I would revert back to barking and demanding.

"After dinner, we'll do your dressing change and make sure you can do it by yourself. I'm sure you're anxious to get out of here," I said casually.

"Okay," she replied.

I waited a few beats to see if she would say something else. When she didn't, I continued, "I have a phone if you want to make some calls.

Your friends and family are probably worried about you."

"They knew I was going on a hiking trip and would be gone for a few days," she replied.

"Have you ever ridden on a motorcycle?" I asked.

"What?" she asked, sounding surprised by my question.

When I repeated myself, she shook her head and asked, "Why?"

"You can't hike out of here on your injured leg, so I'll take you to wherever you need to go," I explained.

She looked at her lap and started fiddling with her hands. "Oh, um, that won't be necessary. Besides, I need to look for the pack I dropped when the boars came after me."

"Hate to break it to you, but I already searched the surrounding area. No sign of your pack."

She huffed. "If it's all the same to you, I would like to look for it myself."

I was getting irritated with her. She was clearly lying to me. I watched her go into the bunker with my own damn eyes. I knew for a fact she had been staying there for several weeks, based on the amount of resources that had been used. Since the food was done, I dropped the subject and sat down beside her to eat.

She ate in silence, side-eyeing me through the entire meal. I wouldn't have been able to keep the smirk off my face if my life depended on it. Never turning my head or my eyes in her direction, I asked, "See something you like?"

She squeaked and flinched. "E-excuse me?"

"You keep glancing at me. Why?" I asked, genuinely curious.

"Sorry. I didn't realize I was doing that," she said softly.

Sure she didn't, but I let it go. The woman was a conundrum wrapped in a mystery. The reason behind her repeated glances was the least of my concerns.

After dinner, we went up to the bedroom to change the dressing on her leg since that's where Splint left an obnoxious amount of supplies. It was also because I planned to resume my quest for answers, and I could easily prevent her from escaping by locking the door. While she was incoherent from the infection, I installed a deadbolt lock on the bedroom as well as locks requiring a key on the bedroom and bathroom windows. She wasn't going to get away from me again.

She went into the bathroom to change clothes, emerging in a tight black tank top and a pair of shorts that were damn near indecent. My cock twitched in my pants. He didn't care about the potential disasters surrounding this woman. All he cared about were the creamy thighs and swells of large breasts on display.

I cleared my throat, "Ready when you are."

She nodded and moved to the bed. "I've already washed my hands," she informed me before silently going through the steps and changing her dressing without issue.

"Good job," I said flatly, causing her head to shoot up. "Now, I'm tired of your bullshit. I want some answers, and you aren't leaving this place until I get them. Are we clear?"

She audibly swallowed and nodded. "What do you want to know?"

"First of all, I want the truth this time. I know you weren't out hiking. I watched you climb out of the bathroom window, slide down a blanket, and walk straight to the bunker. Then, I watched you climb out with two bags, walk off into the forest, and set up a campsite about a mile from here. I also know someone has been staying in the bunker for what appears to be several weeks. I'm guessing that someone is you. So, tell me, Kayla, what the hell are you up to?"

I was not prepared for her response. She blinked her big, blue eyes at me and burst into tears. Sobs and gasps wracked her body as she unleashed a torrent of emotions. Without thinking, I was by her side and wrapping my arms around her. I gently rocked her while smoothing her hair, hoping I was providing some semblance of comfort. Women and their fucking tears.

"Hey, it's going to be okay. You're not in any trouble for being here. No one's going to hurt you. We just want to know what's going on," I murmured.

"We?" she choked out.

"This is my friend's cabin. He lets me stay here when I need a few days away. When I saw you go into the bunker, I thought maybe he forgot to tell me he had a guest. I called and asked, and he didn't have a clue who you were," I explained.

She pulled away from me with a look of horror on her face. "Your friend keeps women in that bunker?" she screeched.

"No! That's not what I meant. The bunker is

more of...a safe house, you could say; a place for someone to stay until it's safe for them to return to their normal life."

She eyed me warily.

I pinched the bridge of my nose, feeling a headache coming on. "I'm not explaining this well. Almost two years ago, a woman, my cousin, had a bad man after her. She came up here to hide out until the bad guy was caught. While she was here, she did have to take cover in the bunker. To my knowledge, that's the only time it's actually been used."

"Is your cousin safe now?" she asked.

"Yes, she is. She's happily married and expecting her first child," I said, smiling at the thought of Ember. She was beautiful inside and out.

"What happened to the bad guy?" she asked.

"He was caught and detained. He died not that long ago," I said, not lying, but not in any way telling her the truth. She didn't need to know the whole story when she was only looking for reassurance.

I gave her a moment to process what I said before gently asking, "Will you tell me how you ended up in the bunker?"

6

LAYLA

"Will you tell me how you ended up in the bunker?" he asked softly.

I couldn't tell him the truth, not all of it anyway. I could give him partial truths and hope it would suffice. I felt like I had a better chance of my plan working if I let him ask the questions instead of volunteering the information. I wasn't a great liar to begin with, and I needed all the help I could get.

"I don't even know where to begin. It's a long story, and one I'm not fond of telling…" I trailed off, hoping he would take that as his cue to lead the conversation.

He rubbed his chin with his thumb and

forefinger before nodding. "Okay, let's start with you answering some of my questions."

I sighed with relief and nodded.

"How long have you been staying in the bunker?"

Of course, he would start off with a question I couldn't easily answer. "Um, what's today's date?"

He gave me an incredulous look before glancing at his phone. "It's February 17th."

"Oh, well, I guess I've been staying in the bunker for four weeks...maybe four and a half," I said distractedly. I was a little taken aback by the date. I knew a good bit of time had passed since the beginning of my nightmare, but I didn't think it had been four weeks.

His mouth opened like he was going to speak, and then he quickly closed it. He did that once more before finally uttering, "Four and a half weeks?"

I felt my cheeks heat in embarrassment. "I didn't realize it had been that long," I hedged.

"Okay, okay, we'll come back to that. How did you find the bunker?"

"Honestly, I stumbled upon it. I wasn't watching the ground, and I literally tripped on the hatch."

"You were out for a stroll in a mountain forest and just happened to trip over an underground bunker?" he asked, clearly not believing me.

I sighed, "I was running and not watching where I was going. I thought something was chasing me."

"Seems like things are frequently chasing you," he muttered.

"Tell me about it," I mumbled. "I swear, I was only trying to get away from whatever was chasing me. When I tripped, I fell onto my hands and knees. That's when I noticed the door. The only thing on my mind was getting away, so I yanked the door open and climbed inside. I had no idea what was down there."

"Once whatever was chasing you was gone, why didn't you leave?" he asked. A valid question. One I couldn't, or wouldn't, answer.

I twisted my hands in my lap while my mind raced to come up with a sufficient answer. "When I found the bunker, it was getting dark, so that's why I initially stayed. The next day, I was scared to leave. When I finally got the courage to come out, the ground was covered in at least a foot of snow. At that point, I had to stay." I paused for a few beats to gather my thoughts. "I was trying to get to the bottom of the mountain when the boars chased me. I don't know what I've done to piss off the universe, but the past year of my life has been a series of devastating events, each one more damning than the last."

"I see," he said, I think more to himself than to me. "Why did you walk a mile and pitch a tent the morning after I found you?"

That one I could answer with the whole truth. "I only walked a mile because my leg was killing me, and I physically couldn't go any farther. I planned to work my way down the mountain, little by little each day and camp at night."

We sat in silence for a few minutes before he asked the dreaded question. "What were you going to do when you got to the bottom?"

"Uh, I was going to see if I could find a ride to a friend's place."

"Well, I can take you to your friend's place, say, maybe day after tomorrow? Give that leg one more day to heal," he suggested.

I tried with everything I had to keep my face neutral and hold back the tears, but I failed miserably. First my chin wobbled, then my lip quivered. Once my nose scrunched, there was no stopping the tears. "I don't know how to get there," I whispered. "I was hoping someone from town would know. I have to find her cabin. I just have to. I don't have anywhere else to go."

He made a humming noise in his throat as his arms surrounded me again. He let me cry for a bit before patting my back and saying, "Don't worry, Locks. We'll find your friend's place." After a few more minutes, he added, "I think that's enough talking for tonight. You need to get some rest."

He stood and moved toward the door, but he stopped at the threshold and turned back, "I won't lock you in here if you promise not to run away."

"I won't. I promise." And I wouldn't. When I told him I didn't have anywhere to go, it was the truth. With not one, but three people looking for me, my options were beyond limited.

THE FOLLOWING MORNING, I PUT ON MY BIG GIRL panties and made myself go downstairs for breakfast. Copper was at the stove with his back to me, his bare back. His well-defined, muscular, mouthwatering back. My hands itched to trace the lines of the tattoos covering most of the exposed skin I could see.

Then, he turned around. And my jaw dropped. His chiseled chest and tapered waist were covered in ink, but his carved abs were bare. His jeans hung deliciously low on his hips, making it clear he was sporting the desired V so many women craved and very few men had.

When I finally managed to drag my eyes away from his sinful torso to his face, he wasn't watching me ogle him. No, he was doing his own ogling, and if my guess was correct, his eyes were fixated on my chest. I cleared my throat, "My eyes are up here, buddy."

He smirked, "I know they are, Locks, but I'm enjoying looking at your tits right now."

I immediately crossed my arms over my chest and scoffed, "I can't believe you just said that to me."

"Why? You're the one who came downstairs with those babies on full display. You don't see me complaining about you staring at my chest, do you?" he said with a smirk and turned back to the stove.

Part of me wanted to dash upstairs and put on the bra I forgot to don while putting on my big girl panties, as well as another shirt. The other part of me was thrilled that he was looking, and enjoying it as he proclaimed. The man was insanely hot, as in way out of my league hot.

"If you're finished brooding, breakfast is ready."

Yes, he was insanely hot, until he opened his mouth and ruined the façade.

"I hope your cooking skills are better honed than your social skills," I muttered, stomping with one foot to the barstool to take a seat.

"Everything about me is well honed, Locks," he murmured, entirely too close to my ear.

"I'll take your word for it," I retorted and shoved a bite of food into my mouth. Damn him and his good cooking for making a moan of appreciation escape from me.

I looked up to find him frozen mid-step, staring at me. I looked down my body and back up to him. "What?" I asked, unsure of what his deal was.

He shook his head and slowly made his way to the bar. "Nothing."

Okay, then. I'm not sure when the dynamic between us changed, but there was an almost palpable tension in the air. I was a firm believer in communication. So, instead of ignoring the issue and allowing it to fester, I asked, "Have I done something to piss you off more?"

He snorted and shook his head. "I don't think so. Why do you ask?"

"I thought I sensed some tension between us. I guess I was wrong," I said.

He laughed as he stood to take his plate to the sink. "No, Locks, you weren't wrong." With that, he rounded the corner and disappeared.

7

COPPER

I was headed for the shower after leaving a stunned Kayla in the kitchen with the intent to relieve some of the tension she was referring to when my phone rang. Phoenix's name flashed on the screen, and I quickly answered, "Phoenix, what's happening?"

He chuckled, "Not a lot. I spoke to Luke last night and sent him the picture. He called this morning and asked for a better picture, closer and with her eyes open. When he ran the one you sent through the database, he got a few hits, but said he could get a more definitive answer from one with her eyes open. He said the closer the better —something about matching color and striations."

"I'll see what I can do. I don't exactly want her to know what I'm doing," I replied. "Regardless, please thank him for me."

"Will do. Oh, almost forgot. He did mention none of the hits he got were named Kayla. There was a Layla and a Kayleigh, but those were the only two similar to Kayla that matched the picture. Are you sure she gave you the correct name?"

"No, man, I'm not. Thus far, she's proved to be a crafty little thing. Wouldn't surprise me if she gave me a fake name."

"All right, man, send that picture to me if you can manage to get one. Talk to you later," he said and disconnected.

That woman was going to cause me to have a stroke before all was said and done. I didn't know if I should be pissed off or proud of her giving me a fake name. I hadn't confirmed it yet, but I knew in my gut that Kayla was not her name, and there was no time like the present to find out.

She was in the kitchen washing our dishes from breakfast when I approached her from behind. Keeping my body out of her line of sight in case she turned around, I softly said, "Kayla." Her head came up, like she thought she heard something, but she didn't bother looking around. I waited a few beats and softly said, "Kayleigh." Again, she lifted her head, this time looking to the side before going back to the dishes. After a few more beats, I said in the same tone and volume I used for the previous two names, "Layla."

Her head whipped up, and she looked to her left, then right, before turning around to look behind her. Could she have turned around because she thought she was hearing things and the third time was the charm? Yes. Did I believe that? Not for one second.

I silently backed away and returned to my room. All thoughts of a tension-relieving shower had vanished into thin air. I didn't want to get myself off to images of a woman who I knew was lying to me. No, I was going to wait for an hour or so and try the name game again. Only this time, I was going to start with Layla to see what kind of response I got. In the meantime, I needed to figure out how to get a decent picture of her without her knowing.

The opportunity presented itself sooner than I thought. The cabin's floor plan was somewhat open. From upstairs, the living room and kitchen were in clear view. She was still in the kitchen, staring out across the living room, seemingly lost in thought. I pulled out my phone, zoomed in, and quickly snapped a picture of her. It looked like a decent picture to me, so I quickly sent it on to Phoenix.

At that point, I was debating whether I should wait to hear back from Luke or forge ahead with my name theory. On one hand, I was dying to know the truth. On the other, I didn't want to spook her and have to deal with her trying to run away again. Especially after she admitted having nowhere to go.

I spent a few hours in my room, mulling over what to do next, before I ventured downstairs for something to eat. Expecting to see Kayla curled up on the couch or sitting at the bar in the kitchen, I was surprised to find her outside on the deck. She was leaning against the railing, gazing at the breathtaking view. Upon closer inspection, I could see the pain and despair on her face. She had a story, and I had no doubt it was not a pleasant one.

I approached her, making enough noise to ensure she heard me coming, and placed my hands on the railing on either side of her, effectively caging her in. She stiffened, but made no move to extract herself. "Beautiful, isn't it?"

She exhaled slowly. "Yes, it is. It's so quiet and peaceful here. I haven't had a lot of that in my life, and I think I'm going to miss it."

"I can understand that. It's the same reason I come up here for a few days whenever I have the time."

I don't know how long we stood in a comfortable silence, enjoying the serenity only nature can offer. It could have been mere minutes as easily as it could have been hours. At some point, she relaxed and leaned back against my chest. I forced my hands to stay on the railing, even though I desperately wanted to wrap my arms around her.

She was maddening, even more so because it was unintentional. One moment I wanted to strangle her, and the next I wanted to smother her body with mine.

Our quiet moment was interrupted by my phone ringing. Expecting it to be Phoenix with an update from Luke, I was surprised to see Judge's name on the screen. Suddenly, I had a sinking feeling in the pit of my stomach. The boys knew not to call and interrupt my brief hiatus. The only one who should call was Bronze, my blood brother and my VP, and only if it was an emergency. I stepped away from Kayla and answered.

"Prez, you gotta get your ass back here now! The clubhouse was attacked. It's bad, brother. The place is swamped with cops and first responders," Judge shouted into the phone.

"Fuck!" I shouted. "I'm heading out now. Was anyone hurt?"

There was a pause, and I knew. I knew why Judge had called instead of Bronze. "Several, including Bronze. He's alive, but that's all I know. He was one of the first ones taken to the hospital," Judge said.

"I'm leaving now. Call Phoenix and ask him to go to the hospital until I can get there. You're in charge until I arrive. Stay safe, brother."

I whirled around and found Kayla staring at me with wide eyes. "I've got to go. There's an emergency back home. I'm not trying to be a dick, but you're coming with me. If you want any of your shit from around here, you have five minutes to get it into a backpack and get your ass on my bike."

She opened her mouth to argue, but I cut her

off. "I don't have time to argue with you. You're going with me. Now, get your shit and let's go!" I barked.

She flinched at my tone and then sprinted for the stairs. Good. I didn't have the patience to deal with her if she tried to argue. My mind was racing. My clubhouse was attacked. My brothers were hurt. My *brother* was hurt. Fuck! I should've asked how bad it was. No, I should have fucking been there instead of off in the mountains trying to clear my head and take care of a random woman with trouble written all over her.

Five minutes later, Kayla came down the stairs with a backpack strapped to her back and silently stood by the back door. I made quick work of locking up and led her to my bike.

As I was strapping my helmet on her head, I told her, "Hold on to me and don't make any sudden movements. Keep your legs and feet away from the pipes. It's usually about a thirty-minute ride, but it's going to be a lot shorter today."

I climbed on and barked, "Get on." She did, and we were off.

8

LAYLA

I was terrified for a variety of reasons. First and foremost, I was riding on a motorcycle for the first time in my life, and it was not a leisurely cruise through the mountainside. No, it was an all-out race at top speeds. All I could do was cling to Copper as tight as I could and keep my eyes squeezed shut. Oh, and pray I didn't puke on his back.

On a positive note, my fear of becoming roadkill was keeping my mind off of venturing back into the world. He never mentioned where exactly we were going. I could only hope it was somewhere no one knew me. I wasn't sure what I would do if it wasn't.

Before long, the bike slowing, coupled with the

scent of smoke in the air, had me cautiously opening my eyes. And immediately slamming them shut.

No.

No.

No.

He was pulling up to a partially burnt building surrounded by flashing lights. And bikers. A lot of bikers. I willed myself not to freak out. I needed to get out of there without drawing any attention to myself. If he thought I was freaking out, he wouldn't let me out of his sight.

Okay, maybe I could play dumb, act like I didn't know this was likely their clubhouse. I could promise to stay put while he did what he needed to do, and when he wasn't paying attention to me, I could sneak away. With a plan in place, I felt better, not much, but a little was better than none at all.

He climbed off the bike and extended his hand to help me. Once I was on my feet, he didn't let go of my hand. Instead, he started speed walking toward a group of bikers, dragging me along in his wake.

"Judge! Update," he ordered.

A large, and might I add extremely good

looking, man turned his head, "Prez." He glanced at his watch and back to Copper. "That was quick."

Did he say 'Prez'? As in President? Oh, fuck me. This was far worse than I thought.

The sexy man called Judge lifted his chin in my direction. "You want me to speak in front of your...guest?"

Copper huffed and grunted, "No." Then, he yanked on my hand and pulled me behind him as he walked up to a woman standing off to the side as if she was waiting for something to do.

"Leigh, this is Kayla, an acquaintance of mine. She's never been here before and doesn't know anyone. Can you watch out for her while I deal with this mess?" he asked, though it didn't sound like much of a question.

She smiled. "Of course. You go do what you need to do. We'll be fine."

With that, he was gone, leaving me standing with a stranger in the middle of a biker compound with a recently destroyed clubhouse. Awkward didn't even begin to cover it.

"What happened to your leg?" Leigh asked.

I jolted at her question, then blinked at her stupidly. "Huh?" I blurted.

She chuckled, "You're a little jumpy. Guess that's understandable considering. Anyway, I was asking what happened to your leg. You've got a noticeable limp."

Oh, crap. What should I tell her? The truth wasn't an option. "Uh, I hurt it while hiking. It's healing well, but I've got an obscene amount of stitches in my calf," I said, hoping she wouldn't ask more questions.

"That sounds painful. Follow me. I'll find somewhere for you to sit and get off of your leg."

I dutifully followed her to an area with several picnic tables. Most were occupied by other women, but one was blessedly available. We took our seats, marking the beginning of an awkward silence between the two of us. I had no idea what to say to the woman. It was clear she was appointed with babysitting me, though she didn't seem to mind.

"So, how do you know Copper?" she asked.

"I don't really know him. He found me when I got hurt and helped me. He let me stay at the cabin for a few days until my leg was well enough for me to get on his motorcycle so he could take me home, which was going to be today, but then all this happened," I said, waving my hand at the general destruction nearby.

"Oh, so you guys just met?" she asked, sounding surprised.

"Yes, about a week ago."

Before she could ask another question, the sexy Judge approached the table at a rapid pace. He placed his hand over his chest and said, "Mom! I've been looking all over for you. Damn near had a heart attack when I couldn't find you."

Leigh was Judge's mother? She didn't look old enough to have a son his age.

"Sorry, son. Copper asked me to watch out for his friend Kayla while he dealt with this mess. She has stitches in her leg, so I brought her over here to sit."

He sighed, "Okay. Let me talk to Copper. I don't want you here until we know it's one hundred percent safe." With that, he turned and disappeared into the mass of people.

"Excuse my son's manners, or lack thereof. He's the SAA for the club and goes by Judge, though he'll always be Jonah to me."

"Wow, you don't look old enough to have a son his age," I blurted.

She smiled brightly. "Thank you. I do believe you're now my new favorite person."

I couldn't help the giggle that escaped me. Something about Leigh put me at ease. She had kind eyes and seemed to have a gentle soul, though I didn't think for one second she would put up with shit from anyone.

I looked up to find her studying me. "Have you been around any motorcycle clubs before?" I shook my head. "Do you know anything about them?"

"Only what I've heard from other people, most of which wasn't positive."

"Yeah, there are a lot of clubs out there that are bad news. This club isn't one of them. These boys make their money legally, and they do what they can to help out in the community," she told me.

"I don't mean to sound rude, but how would you know? I thought it was a general rule that women weren't allowed to know the ins and outs of the club."

She laughed. "I suppose you have a point. For the most part, that's true, but I was married to a member, my son is a member, my nephew is a member, and my niece, who I raised for eight years, is engaged to a member. Plus, I work for the club." When my eyes widened, she quickly added, "I do their bookkeeping. Occasionally, I'll help out with bartending during a party."

"You said you were married. May I ask what happened?"

"My husband, Jonah's father, died in a work-related accident almost fifteen years ago. It happened just before my niece came to live with me. If it weren't for her and Jonah, I don't know how I would've made it through losing him," she said softly.

"I'm sorry. I shouldn't have asked," I mumbled.

She patted my hand. "I'm glad you did. Even though I miss him like crazy, it still brightens my day to think about him. He was a good man, and he lived a full and happy life while he was here."

I was about to comment on how lucky she was to have had a relationship like that when I noticed her attention was focused on something behind me. "Here come the boys," she uttered.

"Mom," Judge rumbled from behind me. "I think it would be better for you to go to the hospital or to your house with a prospect. It's up to you."

"I'd be happy to go to the hospital, but I don't think there's much for me to do right now, other than be in the way. How about I go home for a few hours and then I'll head to the hospital once everyone's been seen and treated?"

"Is that okay with you, Prez?" Judge asked Copper.

Copper nodded, "Leigh, can you take Kayla to your house with you?"

I straightened in my seat, and Copper focused his eyes on me. "Before you start, Judge is right, it's safer for you to be somewhere else until we get to the bottom of this. Leigh doesn't live too far from here, and I'll come get you before I go to the hospital to see about my brother and the other club members."

The next thing I knew, Leigh was driving me to her house with a prospect trailing behind us on his motorcycle.

"What exactly is a prospect?" I asked.

"A prospect is someone who wants to be a member of the club. They have a trial period to prove themselves worthy of membership. It's similar to pledging for a fraternity, but prospecting takes longer and, obviously, is more dangerous," she explained.

"And they trust the new guy to protect us?"

She laughed, "This particular one has been around for almost a year and should be getting his patch soon. Really, it's just a formality to make my son feel better. I can shoot as well as, if not better than, most of the club members."

"What are the chances of something happening to us at your house?" I asked, trying to keep my voice steady.

"There's no reason to be scared. In all the years I've been associated with the club, nothing has ever happened at my personal residence. In fact, I think this may be the first time the club has ever been attacked. I can't say for sure, but I think the attack on the clubhouse was meant to send a message more than it was intended to hurt or kill people. Besides, my son runs a security company. My house is more secure than most government buildings."

We pulled up to a beautiful two-story house situated on several acres of land. There were similar houses on the street, each with a decent sized plot of land, giving the area a neighborhood feel without the congestion of typical subdivisions.

"Are you hungry or thirsty? I'm about ready for something to eat myself," Leigh said.

"I could eat," I hedged. I didn't want to be a burden, but honestly, I was hungry, and I needed to take my medicine for my leg.

"Have a seat and I'll make us some lunch."

We spent the next several hours, eating, talking, and watching television. I don't know if I was giving off a certain vibe, or if I just got lucky, but she didn't ask me any overly personal questions. She kept the topics of conversation light and general, and she would never know just how grateful I was for that.

I was contemplating a nap when Leigh's phone rang. She went into another room to answer it and came back a few minutes later, "Copper wants me to bring you to the hospital."

9

COPPER

It was taking every bit of will power I had to keep myself from exploding. My clubhouse had been attacked. My brother was hurt. Some of my members were hurt. I was already on edge, hence my trip to the cabin. Add Kayla to the mix and I was coiled with a dangerous tension.

After dealing with the local police and answering far too many questions, they finally left the premises. The fire department had been long gone by that point. I didn't even bother scoping out the damage done to the property. As soon as I was free to leave, I went straight to the hospital.

I found Phoenix and a few of the boys from

Croftridge in the Emergency Room waiting room. "How is he?" I asked without preamble.

Phoenix stood and clapped me on the shoulder. "They moved him to a room about an hour ago. I figured you would come to the ER, so that's where I waited for you."

When we stepped into the elevators, he asked, "Where's the girl?"

"Sent her to Leigh's house while I dealt with this shit," I grumbled.

"Does Leigh know to keep an eye on her?"

"Yep. Judge filled her in before they left."

I walked into a hospital room to find my brother resting with his eyes closed. He had some smudges of soot and ash on his face, but otherwise looked okay aside from the bulky bandage covering most of his forearm.

"He's got a significant concussion, which is why he's in a room. They want to keep him overnight for observation. He also has second degree burns on his arm, but those can be cared for at home. As long as he does fine overnight, the doctor said he can be discharged in the morning," Phoenix explained.

"Thanks for coming, man. Any word on the others?" I asked.

"Yeah. Two others are being kept overnight. Everyone else is allowed to go home. I can arrange transportation, just need to know where you want me to take them."

"Who's being kept overnight?"

Phoenix chuckled, "I'm sorry, man. It's not funny, but it is. Two of the club girls." He cleared his throat and continued, "They were in Bronze's room. Both have concussions. One has some burns, and one has a broken arm."

I nodded, "I'll drop in and check on them a little later. I'm going to stay with Bronze for the time being."

"Do you want me to take the rest back to the clubhouse? Is that an option?" Phoenix asked.

"Yeah, take them there. Luckily, only a quarter of the place was sectioned off. The rest of the building was cleared for use."

"All right, I'm going to head back to Croftridge from the clubhouse unless you need me to stay."

"No, you go on back. I know you want to get back to Annabelle."

He smiled proudly. "Indeed, I do."

"How much longer does she have?"

"About six weeks, but twins tend to come early, so it could be any time now."

"Keep me posted. And thanks again," I said.

I dropped my ass into a chair in the corner of Bronze's room and closed my eyes. I just needed a moment to breathe before I continued on with the circus known as my life.

Sighing, I pulled out my phone and called Leigh to have her bring Kayla to the hospital. Before I could put my phone away, it rang in my hand.

"Luke, I didn't expect to hear from you directly," I said, forgoing the standard greeting.

"I figured it was best to cut out the middle man since it sounds like both you and Phoenix are busy. Is now a good time?" he asked.

"Now is probably as good as it's going to get. What'd you find?"

"The picture you sent hit on a Layla East. She's flagged in the database as wanted for questioning related to a current case. Unfortunately, I can't give you much more than that, but I can tell you she's on the victim side of things. We've been trying to locate her for months. I don't know how you found her, but don't do anything to spook her until I can get there."

"And when will that be?" I asked.

"I'm hoping in the next day or two. Is she staying with you?" he asked.

"Not sure I want her at the clubhouse…" I trailed off. I had no doubt he was aware of the attack.

"I can understand that. I hate to ask because I know your plate is full, but can you keep up with her until I can get there. I don't want her turning into a ghost again," he said.

"I'm not going to make any promises, but I'll do the best I can," I said. I couldn't promise him I would keep up with her until he arrived. With everything going on, the clever woman might be able to get away from me. I hoped she wouldn't, but that was for an entirely different reason I was not going to examine until later, much, much later.

"Appreciate it. Like I said, she's on the victim side. I have a feeling she'll stick around as long as she feels safe. I'll let you know when I'm in town," he said and disconnected the call.

Great. I was certain a partially blown up and burned down clubhouse were not on the list of top ten things that would make her feel safe.

Maybe she could stay with Leigh until Luke arrived.

"What are you over there sighing and huffing about?" Bronze croaked from the bed.

I was on my feet and beside his bed in a second. "Bronze, you doing okay?"

"Fuck no! I've got a headache from this damn concussion, my arm feels like it's still on fire, and I've got one hell of a case of blue balls," he grumbled.

I laughed. "I can't help you with that, little brother."

"How bad is the clubhouse?" he asked.

"Not too bad. Only about a quarter of it will have to be rebuilt. Unfortunately, your room is in that section, but we'll figure something out."

"Do we know who was behind it yet?"

"Not yet. Judge didn't see anything on our surveillance cameras, but he only had time to do a quick scan of the feed. Local law enforcement is going to check the security feeds from a few businesses nearby," I explained.

"I don't get it. Why go to the trouble of attacking our clubhouse without letting us know who did it? It doesn't make any sense," Bronze said.

"I agree. Don't worry about it right now. Just focus on getting better. We'll deal with it when we know more. On a different note, Leigh is bringing a new acquaintance of mine up here soon. I'll explain more later, but don't do or say anything to offend or frighten her."

He gave me an appraising look. "Oh, this promises to be a good story."

"You have no idea," I mumbled.

As if on cue, Leigh and the woman I now knew was Layla East walked into the room. And my jaw hit the floor. Layla was wearing a pair of fitted jeans with a tight black t-shirt. The only remarkable thing about her outfit was the way it molded to her body. And it was remarkable. Her long, honey, blonde hair hung in loose curls down her back in stark contrast to the black shirt.

When my eyes landed on her face, I almost choked on my own spit. Leigh had apparently done her makeup, accentuating her big, blue eyes and her plump lips. And holy hell. She looked good.

While I tried to regain some semblance of coherency, Leigh didn't miss a beat. "You like? We were bored, and I convinced Kayla to let me give her a makeover. I haven't had a chance to do one since Harper went off to college."

I cleared my throat and directed my attention to Leigh. "You did a good job."

Leigh swatted my shoulder, "Don't tell me, tell her."

"You look great, Kayla," I rasped. Why was my mouth suddenly dry? I could have sworn I was on the verge of drooling mere seconds ago.

"Thanks," she said softly.

Bronze cleared his throat.

"Oh, you hush. You can handle not being the center of attention for one minute," Leigh playfully scolded him.

"I'm in the freaking hospital. I should be the center of attention," Bronze cried.

"I swear, you're all a bunch of overgrown babies whenever you get sick or hurt," she said. "But I still love you."

"If that were true, I would have one of your homemade cookies in my hand," Bronze said.

Leigh reached into her humongous purse and pulled out a paper bag. She held the sack up and examined it. "Hmm, I'm not sure you deserve these."

"Please, Leigh. You know I didn't mean

anything. I've got a head injury. You can't hold anything that comes out of my mouth against me," Bronze blabbered.

She held the bag just out of his reach, "Only if you promise to share."

"With who?"

"Your brother and Kayla."

"I promise."

She dropped the bag in his lap, and he dove in like a rabid beast. He looked up with a mouthful of cookie and asked, "You guys want some?"

He was met with a chorus of no's.

Shaking my head at my brother, I turned to Kayla, "This is my brother, Bronze. Bronze, this is Kayla."

"Nice to meet you," he said through his mouthful of cookie.

"Uh, likewise. I hope you get well soon," she said, stumbling over her words.

Bronze nodded and continued to inhale Leigh's cookies like he hadn't had any food in days.

"Leigh, Paige and Heidi are in the rooms on either side of Bronze. Would you mind checking in on them? I haven't had a chance to do it myself yet."

Leigh's nose scrunched, but she politely agreed and left the room.

I grabbed Layla's hand and pulled her to the corner of the room. "Would you feel comfortable staying at Leigh's house tonight? I don't want you to stay at the clubhouse, and I don't have time to take you anywhere else."

"Yes, but did you ask her?"

"Not yet, but I know she'll say yes. She's always done whatever she could to help whenever someone asked," I said. Then, an idea popped into my head. "Actually, I might be staying there as well since my room is in the damaged section of the clubhouse." She didn't need to know I had my own place away from the club.

"Okay, whatever you think is best," she agreed, far easier than I expected.

We made small talk until Leigh returned from visiting the girls. As I assumed, Leigh offered her house up to anyone who needed a place to stay. I assured her it would be just the two of us for the time being. She gave me an odd look, but thankfully didn't question why I was staying as well.

10

LAYLA

rap. I didn't want to like these people. I mean, Copper was one hot man, and any heterosexual female would have to agree, but he had been quite a dick to me on more than one occasion.

Leigh, on the other hand, seemed like the older sister I always wished for and never had. She gave me a makeover! No one, not even my own mother, had ever given me a makeover. In Mom's defense, it was probably because she was too busy working her tail off trying to provide a decent life for us.

It would be easier to get away if I didn't like the people. Leigh made me want to stay. And if I was being completely honest, Copper made me want to stay as well, for an entirely different reason.

I knew I couldn't stay. If I did, I could potentially be putting them in danger. I could also be putting myself in danger. I knew there were likely three angry men looking for me, and I had no idea where they were and what connections they had. I couldn't chance being spotted and sent back to one of my previous hells. So, even though I didn't want to leave, I would, but I could stay for a few more days as long as I kept a low profile.

With that decided, I changed into a tank top and some shorts, took care of my dressing, and climbed into bed. It felt like hours before I fell asleep. My mind wouldn't stop running in overdrive.

I woke with a start, my eyes instantly opening and searching for the cause. "It's just me. Didn't mean to scare you," was whispered from behind me.

In. The. Bed.

A warm hand snaked across my waist and pulled me back against a firm chest. "Go back to sleep."

Okay, sure. There's an unexpected man in my bed, but I'll just go back to sleep. I don't think so.

"What are you doing in here?" I asked, my voice hoarse from sleep.

"Trying to get some sleep," Copper grumbled.

"Well, do it in your own bed," I squeaked.

"Sleep, Locks. Just sleep," he mumbled.

Before I could protest any further, his body relaxed and I heard his breathing grow deeper and even out. How in the hell had he fallen asleep that fast?

Much to my chagrin, I found myself snuggling back against him and falling asleep in record time.

When I woke that morning, Copper was plastered to my back, one leg wedged between both of mine, and his hand was cupping my bare breast underneath my tank top. Despite my best efforts to will my body to behave, my traitorous nipples pointed out their delight at the situation.

I took in a slow, deep breath before I tried to extricate myself from Copper's grasp. Unfortunately, I didn't get very far. I had moved maybe an inch when his arm tightened, and by extent, his hand. I involuntarily rolled my hips back, eliciting a low groan from him.

He rocked forward, pressing closer to me and nuzzling my neck, his warm breath causing goosebumps to erupt on my skin. His hand moved down, and he caught my nipple between his thumb and forefinger, pinching lightly. It was my turn to moan. And it might as well have been the equivalent to a bucket of ice water.

Copper was suddenly off the bed and across the room breathing heavily. "This," he barked, pointing an accusatory finger at the bed, "cannot happen." With that, he bolted from the room like his pants were on fire. The bastard even slammed the door on his way out.

To say I was mortified would have been an understatement. Furthermore, I hadn't initiated any of it. He was the one who crawled into bed with me. He was the one who put his hand under my shirt. I tried to spare us both embarrassment by getting out of bed. But HE wouldn't let me.

Well, I was getting out of bed, and I was going to find President Shithead and let him know exactly what I thought about his declaration of what could not happen. Only, I didn't get the chance. Before I could get the door open, I heard a bike fire up and race away from the house. Not only had I driven him from my bed, but I had also driven him from the house as well.

What a wonderful way to start the day. On the bright side, feeling rejected and humiliated would make it easier to leave. On that note, I decided to focus on figuring out how to get to my friend's place. I hated asking people for handouts, but I didn't even have one damn penny to my name, and I refused to compromise my morals for a little bit of money because that would make me just as bad as *them*.

The thought almost had me bursting into tears, until my pity party was interrupted by a knock on the door. Leigh poked her head in and surveyed the room. "I heard Copper roar out of here a few minutes ago. Is everything okay?"

I shrugged, "As far as I know. He didn't say anything to me."

She gave me a once over and pursed her lips. "I see. Well, I was about to start breakfast. You hungry?"

No, I wasn't, but I knew better than to pass up a free meal. My future wouldn't likely hold many full and free meals. I gave her a fake smile, "I am. I just need a few minutes to freshen up."

I let myself have five minutes and no more to silently freak out and break down in the bathroom before I pushed it all to the back of my mind and made my way to the kitchen. Whatever Leigh was making smelled divine.

"Have a seat. It's almost ready," Leigh called over her shoulder.

Minutes later, she placed a loaded plate in front of me, followed by two more full plates, before she sat down with one for herself. Before I could ask, a door opened, and Judge entered the room with another man at his side. A big man. A big, scary man. I briefly wondered if I was to be his snack instead of the food on the table.

Both men took a seat at the table while I continued to stare, frozen in shock. Leigh cleared her throat, "Kayla, I'm not sure if you were formally introduced yesterday. This is my son, Judge. And this big beast might as well be my son. He goes by Batta. Boys, this is Kayla, Copper's friend."

Judge nodded in my direction, "Morning, Kayla."

Batta, who was sitting beside me, held out his hand, "Nice to meet you, Kayla." When my only response was to swallow audibly, he chuckled. "I'm really not that scary, am I?" he asked with feigned surprise.

A laugh burst from my lips before I could stop it, followed by verbal diarrhea. "Hell, yes, you are. You're freaking huge. I mean, really, I didn't know humans came in that size. Were you the size of a toddler when you were born? Oh, your poor mother. Did she survive the birth? Let me see your hand. I bet it's at least half the size of my arm. Oh my gosh, are you like one of those guys on TV that can squat cars and stuff? I can't remember what—"

Batta interrupted me, "Slow down, Speedy, and let me answer one question before you ask another."

I instantly felt my cheeks flame with embarrassment. "I'm so sorry. Sometimes I ramble when I'm nervous. If you'll excuse me, I'll just head upstairs and leave you to finish your breakfast."

His giant hand gently landed on my forearm. "It's fine, sweetheart. Sit and finish your meal. I will say, I've gotten a variety of responses when meeting new people over the years, but yours was by far the best," he said with a twinkle in his eye and laughter in his voice.

I picked up my fork and started eating my breakfast, at a loss for words after my outburst.

Batta, however, was not at a loss for words. "To answer your questions: No, I was not the size of a toddler when I was born. Believe it or not, I was born premature, weighing only three pounds. My mother did survive childbirth and even my teenage years. No, I cannot squat a car, though I can lift the front end of one. And, I believe you were referring to the strongest man competitions. No, I'm not one of those guys," he said, with a cheeky grin.

"You can pick up a car?" I asked incredulously.

"The front end of a car, not a car," he corrected.

"Still, that's impressive. Did you use steroids to get so big?"

He threw his head back and guffawed. "Shit, she's making my eyes water. Leigh, how long is she staying?"

"I don't know, dear. Copper didn't specify when he asked," she replied.

Batta turned his attention back to me, "No steroids. I have a naturally large frame, and I work out regularly. So, how long are you going to be hanging around?"

I tried to mask my panic when I answered, "I'm not sure. I guess until Copper says I can go home."

Batta studied my face and asked, "Why does Copper have any say in when you can go home?"

I dropped my eyes to the plate of food in front of me. "It's a long story, but the short version is, he's helping me with something."

Batta nodded, "I see. Anything I can do to help?"

And just like that, another person had me wanting to stay when I knew I couldn't. I smiled softly, "Thank you for the offer, but unless you can speed up time, there's nothing you can do." His eyebrows crinkled in confusion, so I continued, "I was injured while hiking, and Copper found me. He helped me get the medical attention I needed and has been helping me take care of my leg while it's healing."

"Sounds like Copper," he chuckled. "What happened to your leg?"

"Uh, like I said, I was hiking, and I stumbled upon two wild boars. They charged. I ran. One got the back of my calf before I could get away."

"No shit," he said and gave a low whistle. "That had to hurt."

"Actually, I didn't notice it until after Copper found me. I climbed on top of a large boulder to get away. I figured the boars would eventually get bored and leave, allowing me to get away. Wrong. I was stuck on that rock for a long time before Copper happened to come along. He shot the boars and helped me down. I didn't feel anything until Copper pointed out the blood."

He raised his eyebrows, "Adrenaline can do some crazy things. I hope this doesn't offend you, but can I see it, the wound that is?"

I scrunched my nose, "Yeah, but fair warning, it's nasty." I scooted my chair away from the table and rolled up the leg of my yoga pants to reveal the covered wound. "It's time for me to change the bandage anyway," I said before removing the dressing.

"That little fucker got you good. How many stitches you got in there?"

I shrugged, "I have no idea. I was out when it was sewn up and never bothered to ask."

He nodded, "It looks like it's healing well. How long has it been since it happened?"

I wasn't entirely sure of the answer since I lost a few days with the fever and infection. "About a week, I think. I started running a high fever, so a couple of days are kind of a blur."

"It's looking good now, and you've got one hell

of a story to tell," Batta said with an almost envious tone.

"So, what do you boys have on the agenda today?" Leigh asked as she began clearing the dishes from the table.

"The fire marshal gave us the okay to get started on repairing the clubhouse, so Copper wants all hands on deck. I'm guessing we'll be there all day," Judge answered.

"Is there anything I can do to help?" Leigh asked.

Judge nodded. "Can you pick up the girls and Bronze from the hospital in a couple of hours?"

"Yes, I can do that, but what are you not telling me?" Leigh asked, quirking a brow.

"Bronze and the girls need a place to stay until we can sort something else out," Judge said quickly.

Leigh sucked in a sharp breath, straightened her spine, and placed her balled fists on her hips, "I don't know what you think you have sorted now, but it damn well better not be my house. I'll be happy to pick them up and drop them off somewhere. My house has always been open to the members and their families, not to the club whores. If Bronze wants to crash here, that's fine.

As far as I'm concerned, the girls can stay at Copper's place or he can put them up in a hotel, but they will not stay in my house."

There were so many things in her little rant that warranted further discussion. First, club whores? Second, Copper's place? Copper had his own place, and he was going to have whores staying there for the foreseeable future? I felt a pang of jealousy at the thought, but I put forth my best effort to ignore it.

I had no claim on Copper. Yes, he was attractive, extremely so, but I was planning on leaving in a few days. He could do whatever he wanted with whomever he wanted, especially since he made it clear he didn't want to do whatever with me.

I stood quickly and carried my plate to the sink where I began to wash the dishes while Leigh argued with her son. I made quick work of the dishes and went back to my room before being noticed.

I plopped down on the bed, my shoulders sagging in despair. How had my life turned into such a mess? I was a good person. I followed the law and tried to help others when I could. I didn't use drugs or torture animals. Still, the universe saw fit to take a huge dump on my life starting with my mother's untimely death.

Once the first tear fell, there was no stopping the others. The floodgates opened, and for the first time since the snowball started rolling, I let it all out. I ended up going into the bathroom and turning on the shower to mask my choking sobs. Right there, on Leigh's guest bathroom floor, I cried until I couldn't cry any more.

11

COPPER

My chest tightened when I saw Leigh's name flashing on my cell phone's screen. "Hey, Leigh. Is everything okay?"

"No, Copper, everything is not okay. For the record, I'm talking to you as the little boy who used to run around with my son and get into trouble, not as the President of the Blackwings MC. Having said that, you know good and damn well I wouldn't allow the club whores to stay in my house. That has never been and never will be acceptable. Bronze is more than welcome to stay with the stipulation that he will not bring whores into my home. I'm willing to pick them up from the hospital, but I need you to tell me where to drop them off. Let me know what you decide. Next up, I want to know what in the hell you did to that girl this morning. She ran upstairs after breakfast and locked herself in the guest bathroom. I've had to listen to her cry, and I mean really cry, for over an hour now. Given the way you tore out of here this morning, after sleeping in her bed, it wasn't hard to figure out where to place the blame. On second thought, I don't want to know what you did; just get your ass over here and fix whatever you screwed up."

I waited for more. When nothing came, I pulled the phone from my ear and looked at the screen. She hung up on me. She chewed me a new one and hung up on me. Leigh had never laid into me like that, not even when me, Judge, and Bronze stole her car and wrecked it when we were in high school.

I was still staring dumbly at the phone in my hand when my phone came to life again. This time, Luke's name was on the screen.

"I managed to clear my day, and I'm in Devil Springs. Where do you want to meet me with Layla?" he asked.

"Do you know where Leigh Jackson lives?"

"Yes. Is that where Layla is?"

"Yes."

"I'll meet you there," he said and disconnected.

Fuck! It was barely ten o'clock in the morning, and my day had already gone to shit. Unfortunately, I had a strong feeling it was about to get much worse.

Thankfully, I arrived at Leigh's place before Luke. I needed to give Leigh a brief explanation of what was about to happen in case Kayla/Layla didn't handle things well, which I suspected she wouldn't.

Leigh stepped out onto the front porch when she heard me pull into the driveway. Before she could say anything, I started, "I don't have much time, but there's something you need to know. There's more to the story about how I came across Kayla, and I don't have time to explain it. What I can tell you is while I was trying to help her, I was also trying to figure out who she was. Spazz ran her picture through some facial recognition software, and he got a hit on an FBI site. Phoenix asked his friend who's an agent to check into it. Long story short, he's on his way here now to question her. He did say she was a victim they wanted to question, not a criminal they were actively trying to apprehend."

Her mouth dropped open and closed. She did that two more times before snapping it shut and glaring at me. She then whirled around and went back inside the house without saying a single word to me. Leigh was a remarkable woman, but a pissed off Leigh was downright terrifying.

Luke pulled into the driveway a few minutes later. He stepped out of the car, looking every bit the part of a stereotypical federal agent. He approached me with his hand extended, "Copper, good to see you."

I shook his hand. "Good to see you, too. Got anything for me before I go get Kayla?"

"No. I need to talk to her first; then I can talk to you," he replied curtly.

"Excuse me?" I asked, taken aback by his words.

"I need to question her first, or I won't be able to tell you much more than her name because she's the only one with the answers," he explained.

Oh, I guess that made sense. I assumed he already knew a good bit about her. "Okay. Follow me. It might take a few minutes for me to get her to come downstairs. Leigh mentioned she was upset this morning and has been holed up in her room since breakfast."

"That's fine. I have all day," he replied, taking a seat in the living room.

I forced myself up the stairs and to her door. I knocked and was not surprised when there was no answer. After two more rounds of knocking, I announced, "Kayla, if you don't open this door, I will open it myself." Nothing.

I set to work popping the flimsy lock on the door and let myself into the bedroom. She was nowhere to be found. My eyes immediately went to the window, and I sighed in relief when I checked it and found it was still locked. Then, I noticed the bathroom door was closed, and the light was on. Was she legitimately using the facilities or was she trying to hide in the bathroom? I knocked on the door. Again, nothing. I issued my warning once more and was still met with silence. Irritated at that point, I popped the lock on the bathroom door and entered.

She was lying on the bath mat, curled into a ball, sound asleep. Her puffy eyes and tear-stained cheeks did not go unnoticed. I crouched beside her and placed my palm on her cheek, "Kayla, sweetheart, wake up." When she didn't budge, I gently shook her shoulder and said her name a little louder.

Her eyes flew open, and she looked confused for a brief moment before a scowl took over her pretty face. She pushed back from me and sat up. "What are you doing in here?"

"I knocked, and you didn't answer. I was worried something was wrong," I explained.

"Oh, okay. This morning you treat me like a damn leper, and now you're suddenly concerned. Completely rational behavior," she spat.

"I don't have the time or patience to argue with you. I need you to get up and come downstairs with me."

"Why?" she demanded.

"Because I asked you to, okay?"

"Fine," she huffed. She got to her feet, and just like the brat she could be, she stomped down the stairs with her arms crossed and her lips pursed. And then she froze when she reached the bottom. She took one look at Luke and tried to run back up the stairs.

I caught her by her upper arms and held her in place. "Hey, calm down. Do you know who he is?"

She frantically shook her head. "No, but he looks like a cop, or a fed. Let me go, Copper. Now."

"No can do, Locks. He's a friend of mine. You're not in any trouble, and no one is going to hurt you. He just wants to ask you some questions," I explained, making an extra effort to keep my voice soft.

She didn't agree, but she didn't fight me as I carefully guided her down the stairs and to the living room. Once seated, she stared at Luke with wide eyes full of trepidation.

"Hi, I'm Agent Luke Johnson with the FBI. Like Copper said, you're not in any trouble. I'm working on a case, and we have reason to believe you were one of the victims. I'm only here to ask you a few questions in hopes you can help tie up a few loose ends in the investigation. Are you comfortable with Copper staying while we talk or would you prefer to speak privately?"

"You might as well go ahead with him here. If I've learned anything in the last week, it's that he has no respect for boundaries and would likely be listening at the door," she snarked.

"Okay then, let's get started. Is your full name Layla Jade East?"

She sucked in a breath and stiffened. I whispered, "I already know." She jerked her head toward me and met my eyes for a brief moment before answering him. "Yes, that's me."

Luke continued, "Do you know Lawrence Hastings or Harold Hensley?"

I felt every muscle in her body tense. When I glanced down, she was white as a ghost, and I wasn't sure she was breathing. "Layla?" I asked.

She blinked at her name, but showed no signs of moving or answering or breathing. I gently shook her shoulder, "Layla, are you okay?"

She whispered, "Define know."

Luke cleared his throat and softened his voice, "Were Hastings and Hensley planning on selling you?"

I was off the couch and on my feet in a flash. "Are you shitting me?!" I roared.

Luke remained seated and kept his voice level, "Calm down and let her answer the question."

"Yes," she whispered.

"And you managed to escape? Is that correct?"

"Yes."

"How did you get away?" he asked, and by his tone, he seemed to be genuinely curious.

She shrugged, "I used one of the bedsheets to hold some hay above the door. When the guard or whatever came in to deliver my dinner tray, the hay fell on his head. While he was distracted, I slipped out the door and ran."

"Simple, yet effective. Well done," Luke complimented while nodding his head in approval.

"What happened to you while you were there?"

"Nothing, really. I was locked in a stall for horses with a crappy bed. They fed me, occasionally yelled at me, and sprayed me down with a water hose every other day," she said flatly.

"How did you come to be in their possession?"

The small amount she had managed to relax vanished with that question. "Pass," she uttered.

"What?" Luke asked.

"Pass. I don't want to answer that one. Pass," she explained.

"Layla, I'm trying to make sure everyone associated with Hastings and Hensley have been apprehended. Did they take you themselves or were you sold to them?"

She exhaled tiredly, "I was sold to them." She

held up her hand to stop his next question. "Let me save you the trouble. My mother passed away a few months ago. My father, who was never a part of our lives because my mother claimed he was a bad man, showed up at the funeral. He shoved me into a van, restrained me, and took me to some shithole where I was locked in a room for a few days. One day, he came to get me, threw me in a trunk, and sold me to the two pricks at the horse farm."

Luke nodded, leaning forward with rapt attention. "What's your father's name?"

Layla made a disgusted face and spat three words that rocked my world, "Jimmy 'Gnaw' Burnett."

12

LAYLA

The moment I uttered my father's name, the air in the room shifted. And neither man said a word. I looked between their shocked faces and finally demanded, "What?"

Luke came out of his stupor first. "What do you know about your father?"

"Not much, and what I do know my mother told me on her death bed. She said he was part of a gang and a bad man. When she found out she was pregnant with me, she left him and worked her tail off to make a life for us. The first time I met him was when he kidnapped me after the funeral. I'm not sure how he even knew about me. She said she never told him she was pregnant, and he isn't listed on my birth certificate," I explained.

Luke blew out a breath. "Your father is dead," he blurted.

"Good. How did he die?"

"He was shot in a warehouse that blew up. It couldn't be determined if the bullet or the fire killed him first."

"What happened to the person who shot him?" I asked.

"We don't know who shot him. Why?" Luke asked with a furrowed brow.

"I wanted to know who to thank," I said, meaning every word. "So, do you have any other good news for me?"

Luke grinned, "Hastings and Hensley have been arrested and are currently in custody awaiting trial. We'd been investigating them for a while. Actually, I was posing as a buyer and set to purchase you, but you managed to get away, which threw a wrench into our plans. In the end, it all worked out, and we got both of them."

"I'll fill her in on the other details," Copper said cryptically.

Luke nodded, "Of course. Only a few more things to clear up, and I'll get out of your hair.

Where have you been since you got away from Hastings? We haven't been able to find a trace of you since you got away from the stables."

I tensed. I didn't want to tell him where I'd been before I found the bunker. Thankfully, I didn't have to because Copper took care of it for me. "Believe it or not, she stumbled across Badger's bunker and has been holed up there until I found her last week."

"How the hell did you get into that thing?" Luke asked.

I shrugged, "It was unlocked."

His brows rose, and his eyes shot to Copper. "When Ember was at the cabin with Dash, we apparently forgot to lock the bunker when all was said and done. Afterward, no one thought to check it."

Luke shook his head in disbelief. "Okay, I think I have what I need. What's the best way to get in touch with you? I may have more questions, but we'll definitely need you to testify at the trial."

"You can call me until I can get her a phone," Copper answered.

We shook hands and said our goodbyes. Once Luke was gone, I faced Copper. "What are the other details?"

"Let's go upstairs, and I'll tell you."

The last thing I wanted to do was go upstairs with him after his behavior that morning, but I desperately wanted to know whatever details he had to share.

He closed the door and took a seat beside me on the bed. "First, I have a question or two for you. I can't believe I didn't think of it earlier, but with the way we met...Anyway, how did you get from the Senator's place in Kentucky to Meadow Ridge? And don't bullshit me. I know you didn't walk."

I swallowed thickly. "You're right. I didn't walk, but I don't feel comfortable telling you that story," I confessed.

His forehead scrunched while he stared at me for a few seconds before his eyes widened as something occurred to him. "You said you were running from something that was chasing you, but it wasn't something, was it? It was someone."

I DIDN'T KNOW WHAT TO DO, AND I COULDN'T STOP crying. I had no idea where I was, and it was starting to get dark. My feet were killing me, I was exhausted, and I

could hardly swallow because my mouth was so dry, but I couldn't stop moving.

When I heard a car approaching, I darted off into the trees to hide until it passed. But it didn't pass. Instead, the car came to a stop, and someone got out. My heart pounded in my chest as I heard footsteps getting closer to the tree I was tucked behind.

"Hello?" an elderly female voice called. "You looked like you could use some help, sweetheart. You still there?"

I fought to silence my breathing while my heart worked overtime in my chest.

"Can I give you a ride somewhere? It's not safe to be walking out here at night, honey. We've got a lot of wild animals around here that like to come out after dark, and I can't in good conscience leave you here," she continued. "I'm a God-fearing Christian woman, but I don't pass judgment. I'll take you wherever you want to go, no questions asked."

What was I supposed to do? She was right about the animals. I had already heard several coyotes howling in the distance. But what if it was a trap? What if she was sent to find me and bring me back?

"Name's Evelyn Carmichael. I'm a seventy-two-year-old widow. I live about an hour from here. Just passing through on my way home from my sister's funeral. It'd sure brighten my day if you'd let me help you."

Taking a deep breath, I prayed she was being honest and stepped out from behind the tree.

She gasped and covered her mouth with her hand. "Oh, honey, I don't know what happened, and you don't have to tell me, but please let me help you."

I swallowed with what little saliva I had and managed to say, "I could use a ride."

"Of course, sweetheart. Hop in the truck."

True to her word, she didn't ask about how I came to be in my current situation. She gave me a few minutes to myself before asking, "Where would you like to go?"

If that wasn't the million-dollar question, then I didn't know what was. I couldn't go home, and the one person I could always count on was gone. "Um, is there a women's shelter nearby? Or something like that?"

She made a sound of discontent with her teeth. "I don't rightly know. I live in Meadow Ridge, about half-way up the mountain, and I know we don't have one in our little town. I suppose there might be something like that in one of the bigger cities, but I'm afraid we won't get you there before they close their doors tonight."

"I don't have anywhere else to go," I blurted, trying not to panic and epically failing.

"Of course, you do, sweetheart. You can spend the night at my place. I have a guest bedroom, and you'd be doing me a favor by keeping me company. I used to spend my evenings talking to my sister on the telephone, right up until the night before she passed. I've been up at her place ever since, so this'll be my first night back in my own house. I was wondering what I was going to do with myself when I spotted you jumping into the trees. It was like the good Lord heard me and answered my prayers right then and there."

"I, I don't—" I started, but she knew what I was going to say.

"Just say, 'Okay,' sweetie," she prompted.

"Okay, Mrs. Carmichael. Thank you."

"Psshaw, you can call me Evelyn. Mrs. Carmichael makes me sound old."

I couldn't help but laugh.

After a few minutes of silence, she finally asked, "What should I call you?"

"Kayla. Kayla West," I lied. It wasn't in my nature to outright lie to people, but I couldn't risk being found.

Evelyn turned out to be my saving grace. After making something for us to eat, she showed me to her guest room, which had an attached bathroom. She went to bed right after dinner, and I took the opportunity to wash off and soak my sore feet in the tub.

The next morning, the unmistakable smell of a home-cooked breakfast and fresh coffee woke me. My feet were killing me, but I managed to wobble out to the kitchen to find Evelyn piling food onto a plate. "You're just in time. Have a seat," she said and nodded to the table which already had a plate of food and two mugs of coffee on it.

"How are you feeling this morning? And don't say fine. There's no way you're fine, so go ahead and be honest," she said before tentatively taking a sip of her coffee.

"My feet hurt, and my legs are a bit sore, but I think I'm okay otherwise."

She huffed and got up from the table. "I don't know where my brain is most of the time. Ah, here we go. Take a couple of these and help yourself if you need more later," she said and placed a bottle of ibuprofen in front of me.

"Thank you," I replied quietly and swallowed two tablets.

"So, I spent a little time last night thinking and praying about you, and here's what me and the Lord came up with. I think you ought to stay with me for a spell. I'm old, and my health ain't all that great. I sure could use some help around this place. I want to get it cleaned out and fixed up so I can sell it and move to a retirement community like all the other old folks are doing. Might even get me a new hairdo and see if I can snag me a fella, maybe even two," she said with a mischievous grin.

After a little more convincing, I finally agreed to stay with Evelyn and help her get her house ready to sell. She even insisted on paying me for the work I did. I didn't want to take her money and tried to refuse, but she told me she was planning on hiring a company to do it, so if I didn't take her money, someone else would.

We spent the next eight weeks diligently working on her house. The woman had an unbelievable amount of stuff. I honestly wasn't sure we would ever get it cleaned out, but we kept at it and made progress little by little.

Each week, Evelyn made two trips into town; one was to take a load of items to be donated, and the other was to take a load of items to the dump. I was scared to go into town, but I knew she couldn't unload the truck by herself, so I offered to go with her. She knew I was scared and hiding from something, but, true to her word, she never tried to pry.

"There's no need for you to tag along. There's plenty of young men around who won't let me lift a finger," she assured me.

It usually took her a little over three hours round trip, but sometimes longer if she needed to stop by the grocery store or the pharmacy. So, when I heard her pull up to the house less than an hour after she left, I automatically thought something was wrong. And I was right.

It wasn't Evelyn and her truck in the driveway. It was a man I'd never seen before, and he did not look the least bit friendly. He knocked on the front door and immediately tried turning the knob. Without giving it any thought, I moved as fast as I could to the guest bedroom and threw myself into the closet. It wasn't big by any means, but I managed to wedge myself behind some of the hanging clothes.

I heard a door crash open followed by clomping footsteps. "Ma, you home?" he called out, and I knew who was inside the house, Evelyn's son, Travis. She told me all about him within the first few days I was with her.

"He's my son, and for that, I will always love him, but that doesn't mean I'm blind to what he's become. To put it bluntly, he's a drug addict who has no desire to change his ways. He's been to jail so many times I've lost count, but he goes right back to his old habits as soon as he gets out. Last I heard, he was supposed to be locked up for three years in the state prison, but half the time they get out of it by telling on somebody else. Honestly, my husband and I washed our hands of him years ago, and I don't bother trying to keep up with him anymore."

He continued moving through the house. I could hear drawers being opened and closed, things being rummaged through and dumped onto the floor. Hopefully, he would find whatever he was looking for and leave before Evelyn got back. She didn't say as much, but I was afraid he would hurt her.

What I didn't expect was him to fling open the closet door and immediately spot me. "Well, what do we have here?" he said as he wrapped his clammy hand around my arm and pulled me from my hiding place.

"I-I'm your mother's friend. P-please don't hurt me," I blabbered.

"Mom's been talking about me, huh? The old bitch never could keep her fat mouth shut," he grumbled and slapped me across the face.

I stumbled back, cupping my stinging cheek. "N-no, she didn't say anything about you. I heard you call her 'Ma' when you came in."

"Shut up, bitch," he ordered and started advancing on me, staring at me with cold, beady eyes.

I didn't have anywhere to go. He was blocking the only exit, and I didn't think I could get around him. I went for the bathroom, hoping I could close the door and lock it to keep him out, but I wasn't fast enough.

He grabbed my shirt and yanked me back until I hit his chest. His rancid smell singed my nose as his hot breath puffed against the shell of my ear. "Where do you think you're going? I want to have a little fun with you."

When his hands moved over my breasts, I turned quickly and shoved against his chest as hard as I could. He only took one step back before he came at me again, roughly pushing me onto the bed and coming down on top of me. I tried to scoot away, but he was too heavy, and I didn't get very far.

As he wrestled with my clothes, I fought him with everything I had. He reared back and slammed his fist into the side of my head causing my vision to blur. My arms were flailing, trying to deflect another hit, when my fingers brushed against something familiar. With zero hesitation, I wrapped my hand around it, swung my arm in an arc over my head, and plunged Evelyn's knitting needle into his eye.

For a split second, he froze in horror. I, however, did not. I used that moment to shove him off of me and get the hell out of there. I ran through the house and crashed through the back door, hitting the ground at a full sprint.

"You fucking bitch," he roared from somewhere behind me, but I didn't dare turn my head to look back. No, I kept running until I physically couldn't run anymore. Only then did I turn to look behind me, and sagged in relief when I saw no one in sight. But after taking a few minutes to catch my breath, a new horror dawned on me. Even if I'd wanted to go back to Evelyn's, I couldn't, because I didn't know where in the hell I was.

"THAT'S HOW I FOUND THE BUNKER, AND THAT'S why I was scared to leave. I was going to go back to her cabin, to make sure she was okay, but I didn't know how to get there, and then it snowed.

She wasn't home when her son attacked me, but I've got to make sure she's okay, and let her know that I'm okay. If it wasn't for her, I don't know where I'd be right now," I sobbed.

Copper curled his arm around my shoulders while I cried on his. "My friend, Badger, who owns the cabin and bunker knows Evelyn. He talked to some people from town, and I'm sorry, Locks, but Evelyn's son did hurt her, or I assume it was him. She told the police she fell down her front steps, hitting her head and breaking her hip. She also reported you missing, but refused to give a name and only gave a vague description. The whole story makes more sense now. Sounds like she was trying to protect you."

I gasped in horror and cried harder. "Where is she? I have to go see her!"

"I don't know exactly, but I'll find out. Badger said she'd been in a rehab facility in the city while her hip healed," he told me.

"Did he say anything about her son?" I asked even though I was scared to know the answer.

Copper grimaced and shook his head. "No, he didn't mention anything about her son, but you can damn well rest assured that he will pay for what he did to his mother and tried to do to you," he said vehemently.

"I don't want to cause any trouble. I just want to make sure she's okay and do whatever I can to help her."

"You aren't causing any trouble. He committed a crime, a few actually, and he needs to be punished, just like anyone else who breaks the law."

I cleared my throat, but couldn't bring myself to meet his eyes, "Yes, but, you're the President of a motorcycle club—"

He stopped me with, "Layla, he was going to rape you. He physically injured his mother. Why do you care what happens to him?"

"I don't care what happens to him, but I don't want you to have blood on your hands because of me," I explained.

He chuckled, "I appreciate the concern, but I didn't mean I would deal with him; I was referring to the police."

"Oh, well okay then," I said. "Can you call your friend and find out where Evelyn is?"

"Yeah, I will, but let me fill you in on the other details first. Just like a Band-Aid. Ready?" No, I most certainly was not ready, but I gave him a curt nod anyway.

"You have a half sister named Annabelle. She's married to my cousin, Phoenix."

As a child, from time to time I wondered if whoever my father was had other children, but it was the last thing I expected to hear at that moment. "What?" I breathed.

"You heard me, Locks. I'm sure she'll be thrilled to meet you. She and Phoenix have twins, a boy and a girl, who are nineteen or twenty by now, and she has a boy who's a year younger than them. She's currently pregnant with another set of twins that are due in the next few weeks. Oh, and Ember, their daughter, is also pregnant, but she's only got one in there."

"Does she know about me?" I asked, afraid to hear the answer.

"No way. She would've looked for you if she did. She hated her parents from what I remember. Phoenix and Annabelle are a bit older than me, but from what I learned as an adult, she despised her father."

"Are there any others?"

"Not that any of us know about. I've got a tech guy in the club, and Phoenix has one in his;

we can get the two of them to do some searches and see if anything comes up," he offered.

"Maybe one day. Let me absorb this first," I said distractedly. My mind was whirling—a sister. I had a sister. An older sister. And nieces and nephews. I had a family! My whole life it was just Mom and me. When she died, I felt so alone, which admittedly, had a lot to do with why I wasn't in a rush to return to reality.

"That's fine, but I have to tell Phoenix about you. He's family, and he's also the President of the original chapter of Blackwings. In other words, he's the President of Presidents. I can't keep this from him," Copper said carefully.

"I wouldn't ask you to," I answered truthfully.

"Annabelle will want to meet you as soon as possible. Are you ready for that?" he asked.

Was I? "I don't think anyone is capable of being ready for the news I received today. I mean, it's a lot to take in, but finding out I have a sister isn't exactly bad news."

"I'll call him this afternoon after I give Badger a call about Evelyn. I hate to leave after dropping a bombshell on you like that, but I need to get to the clubhouse and get started on the mess over there. I probably won't be back until later tonight. Are you going to be okay?"

"Don't worry about me. I'll be fine," I said flatly.

"Layla, about this morning——"

I cut him off. "Don't. Let's forget it happened and never mention it again."

"It's not what you think," he continued.

"It doesn't matter what I think. Let it go, okay?"

He nodded once in acknowledgment and dropped a kiss on top of my head. "I'll see you later. Leigh has my number. Don't hesitate to call if you need anything." With that, he left.

I flopped onto my back on the bed and covered my eyes with my hands. I had a sister, my father was dead, and Hastings and Hensley were in custody. That meant only Evelyn's son might be looking for me, but the chances of running into him were slim to none. Was it possible to get my life back? It sounded like it might be, but I was too afraid to let my mind go there.

13

COPPER

When I arrived at the clubhouse, Judge, Batta, and most of the other brothers were already working on the damaged section of the building. "I'll be there in a few," I called out as I walked to my office.

I figured it was better to call Phoenix sooner than later. If Luke said something to him before I did, he would have my ass. "Phoenix Black," he barked into the phone.

"Got a minute?" I asked.

"Yeah. I'm in my office. What's up?"

"Luke dropped in this morning to question the girl I found squatting in Badger's bunker. Turns out she was kidnapped by her estranged father at her mother's funeral and sold to Hastings and Hensley. She managed to escape without a trace and stayed with a friend for a while, but shit happened there that caused her to run, which is how she stumbled upon the cabin and the bunker."

"Holy shit, man. So, she had no idea Hastings and Hensley had been arrested?"

"Nope. She thought they'd be looking for her, as well as her father."

"What kind of man does that to his own daughter? Tell me that asshole was arrested with the rest of them," he said.

"He wasn't. He was killed before his involvement with Hastings and Hensley was discovered," I hedged.

"Quit beating around the bush, Copper. What are you not telling me?"

I sighed, "The woman's name is Layla East, and her father's name is Jimmy 'Gnaw' Burnett."

Silence.

"Phoenix?"

More silence.

I checked the phone to make sure I hadn't dropped the call.

"Phoenix?"

"Fuck," he breathed. "She's Annabelle's sister."

"Yeah, she is. That's why I'm calling," I said. "I figured Annabelle would want to meet her as soon as possible. I know Layla wants to meet her."

"Did she know about Annabelle?"

I chuckled, "Layla asked the same thing. And, no, she had no idea of Annabelle's existence. She didn't even know who her father was until her mother told her right before she died a few months ago."

"If I share this news with Annabelle, she is going to insist on meeting her right away, and she's in no shape to travel. Honestly, the excitement might not be good for the babies. I hate to say it, but I think it would be best to wait until after she delivers to share this news with her. Do you think Layla will agree to that?"

"I don't see why not. I don't know her very well, but she seems like a kind and understanding person who has been handed more than her fair share of bullshit in her lifetime," I said. "You know, when I first saw her, there was something familiar about her that I couldn't place. Knowing what I know now, it's obvious. She reminded me of Annabelle."

"How old is she?" Phoenix asked.

I chuckled, "I don't know for sure. It never occurred to me to ask, but I'd guess she's around twenty-four or twenty-five years old."

"What are her plans now? Does she have a home or family to get back to?"

"We haven't talked about it in great detail, but once or twice she mentioned she didn't have anywhere to go. I'm guessing wherever she did live is probably long gone by now since she was MIA for so long. Same goes for whatever job she had, too. She did say that her mother died right before Gnaw took her, but she hasn't mentioned any other family," I replied.

"Let me know what she needs, and I'll take care of it. Annabelle isn't going to be happy when she finds out I kept this from her, but she would have my ass if I didn't take care of her sister."

Not happening. If anyone was going to take care of Layla, it was going to be me. "Don't worry about it. You've got enough on your plate for the next few weeks. I'll take care of Layla for the time being," I offered.

"Thanks, man. I appreciate it," he said. "Any updates on the attack?"

"Nothing, yet. I'll be sure to let you know if

anything comes up." We talked for a few more minutes before ending the call.

The next few hours were spent helping my brothers sort through the massive pile of rubble and debris that was once part of our clubhouse only to find very little worth saving. When we stopped for a bite to eat, Judge left to start reviewing the security footage. Spazz went back to his room to start working his magic on his computer. We needed answers yesterday. I wanted to know who attacked my club and why.

Color me surprised when I saw Boar's name flashing on my phone's screen.

"Heard a rumor your club was attacked yesterday. I hope there's no truth to that," Boar rumbled in my ear.

"Wish I could say there wasn't, but that'd be a lie," I replied.

"Fuck, man. Anybody hurt?"

"Bronze and a couple of club whores spent the night in the hospital, but they'll all be okay. A handful had some minor cuts and bruises. Destroyed a quarter of the clubhouse, though."

"Mind if I ask who did it?" he asked.

"That's what shits me about it; I don't have a fucking clue who was behind it. Judge and Spazz are trying to find something to point us in the right direction," I answered honestly. Normally, I wouldn't share club business so freely with another club, but Boar had shockingly proven to be a strong ally for the Blackwings over the last two years. He and his club had been more than willing to step in and lend a hand to Phoenix's club at the drop of a hat on more than one occasion.

His extended silence had the hairs on the back of my neck rising. Finally, he asked, "Are you aware of what went down with the Disciples of Death last week?"

"No. Is there a reason I should be?" I asked warily.

He cleared his throat, and his tone changed to one of a more serious nature. "Listen, Copper, I'm not insinuating anything here; I'm just sharing a bit of information you may or may not find useful." I heard him exhale slowly. "Last week, Scream and his VP, Belch, were killed. From what I've heard, they were taken out by their own club. Word is some guy called Aim took over as the new President, and he handpicked all new officers."

"I see," I said, pinching the bridge of my nose to relieve some pressure. "Do you know why?"

"Nope. Haven't heard a word about their reasoning. I've got my ear to the ground, and I'll let you know if I hear anything else. I could be wrong, but I've got a feeling the new leadership is going to be bad news for anyone in their vicinity."

"Fuck," I cursed. "Seems awfully coincidental my club was attacked a week after new leadership forcefully took over. I didn't have a truce or even a good relationship with Scream, but he didn't fuck with my club."

"Yeah, because the fucker was scared of you and Phoenix. We had some trouble with them years ago, but that wasn't Scream's doing. Seems the trouble he had with rogue members finally got the better of him, so to speak."

"Sounds like it. Listen, I've got to get back to getting shit sorted. Thanks for calling and letting me know about Scream and Belch," I said.

"No problem. I'll let you know if I hear anything else," he said and disconnected.

I headed straight to Spazz's room. As expected, I found him hunched over his computer, his face entirely too close to the screen. "Spazz, I've got something for you." After filling him in on my conversation with Boar, I left him to search for anything and everything he could find on Aim and the new officers of the Disciples of Death.

Finally, I gave Badger a call and told him what Layla shared with me about Evelyn. "She wanted to know if you could find out how to get in touch with Evelyn. She desperately wants to talk to her and make sure she's okay."

"I'll give Madge a call and ask. She keeps up with everyone in town, so if anyone'll know, it'll be her," Badger said.

"Might as well see if she knows anything about Evelyn's piece of shit son while you're at it."

"She probably doesn't, but I'll ask. Travis hasn't been welcome in town since his dad ran him off years ago. The way it was told to me was Archie came home from work one day and found Travis slapping Evelyn around in the kitchen. I only met Archie a few times before he passed, but even in his later years, the man was built like a brick shit house. Anyway, he beat the piss out of Travis and told him never to come back," Badger explained.

"Yeah, Layla said Evelyn told her he was mixed up with drugs and had been in and out of jail many times over the years. I've already got Spazz checking into him, but you know how it goes with small rural towns."

He chuckled. "That I do. You want me to give Sheriff Simmons a call and see if he knows anything?"

"Thanks, but no. I'd like to have a word with him myself before handing him over to the police," I said.

"Understood."

With that, we ended the call, and I tilted my head back and closed my eyes. I needed a vacation.

14

LAYLA

I was in bed, but not asleep, when I heard a light knock on the door. Copper was the only person it could be, and I wasn't sure I wanted to see him. I had been lost in my thoughts the entire day, and I studiously avoided thinking about him, which turned out to be much more difficult than I anticipated.

I stayed perfectly still, hoping he would think I was asleep and leave, but I should have known better. When the man wanted something, he got it. I was all too aware of this when I heard the door creak open. I hadn't bothered with locking it since that hadn't stopped him from entering before.

"Layla," he whispered.

I wanted to keep pretending I was asleep, but that wasn't the mature thing to do. Sighing in exasperation, I forced myself to act like an adult and rolled to my side to face him, "Yes?"

He slowly came closer. "You doing okay?"

"I'm fine," I replied flatly and waited for him to say or do something. When he didn't, I asked, "Did you need something?"

He blinked and nodded, "Uh, yeah. I wanted to let you know I talked to Badger earlier this afternoon. He's going to work on getting a phone number or address for the rehab place where Evelyn is recuperating."

"Thank you." I felt a small sense of relief knowing I was one step closer to finding Evelyn.

"Also, I spoke with my cousin, Phoenix, earlier today. He thought it would be best to wait to tell Annabelle about you until after she has delivered the twins. She would want to meet you right away, and he doesn't want her traveling this late in the game. Plus, he thought the excitement of the news might not be good for the babies. I hope you're okay with that decision."

"Of course, I am. I certainly don't want anything to happen to her or her babies..." I trailed off, unsure of how to bring up the rest of my concerns.

"What is it?" he asked.

I pushed myself to a sitting position and started fidgeting with my hands. "You mentioned she was due in a few weeks. What happens between now and then?" I asked carefully.

"The club will make sure you have everything you need until then," he stated.

"Excuse me?" I asked incredulously.

"The club will make sure you have a place to stay, food to eat, clothes to wear, and anything else you need," he said.

"No," I stated vehemently. "Absolutely not." I could feel the anger building with each second that passed.

"It's not up for discussion," he informed me.

And that did it. I was on my feet and in his face. "You listen to me, you motherfucker. You can't come in here and tell me the club will take care of me. You will not turn me into a club whore!" I screamed.

He took a step back, confusion evident on his face, "What in the hell are you talking about?"

I took a step forward and jabbed my finger into his chest. "Does the club take care of the club whores? Provide them with food, shelter, clothing, and whatever else they need?"

"Well, yes, but—"

"But nothing. That is not, never has been, and never will be, *me!*"

He circled my wrist and gently pulled my finger from his chest. "Locks," he said, in a patronizing tone I decidedly did not care for.

"Get out!" I yelled and damn near stomped my foot to punctuate it.

"Locks," he said again.

"Get. Out," I gritted out through my clenched jaw.

Still holding my wrist, he gave it a gentle, but firm tug, pulling me flush against his chest. "Shut. Up," he growled and circled my waist with his free arm.

"No fucking way, buddy," I spat, trying, unsuccessfully, to remove myself from his hold.

His free hand cupped the back of my neck, and his fingers slid between the strands of my hair. He tightened his hold and tugged, forcing my head to tilt back. Before anything could register through the anger overtaking my brain, his lips were on mine. And he wasn't gentle. No, he was strong, forceful, demanding, and consuming.

I tried to resist, tried to pull away, but my underlying desire for him was no match for the anger I was feeling moments before. And honestly, I needed the physical connection. It had been so long since I had experienced any kind of positive interaction with anyone, particularly a man.

I melted into him, succumbing to the demands of his lips and tongue. I was lost in his kiss, lost in lust, lost in him. So, when he abruptly pulled back, I was left standing with my mouth hanging open and a look of shock on my face.

"Listen and listen good, woman," he said in a tone that brooked no argument. "I said nothing about you being a club whore. I said the club would take care of you. If you would've let me speak, I would've told you it was because you're family. In case it didn't register to you, you are the sister-in-law of the President of the entire fucking club."

"Oh, ah, oops," I said and shrugged, hoping to lighten the moment, as well as hide my embarrassment from overreacting.

"Oops? That's all you got?" he growled,

stepping forward and forcing me to take a step back.

I cast my eyes to the ceiling, pretending to search my brain for another answer that wasn't there. I looked back to him and said, "That's all I got."

"Woman," he growled. And then I was falling backward, landing on the bed with a bounce and a squeak.

Copper followed me down, hovering over me with his much larger frame, his fists planted beside my shoulders. He lowered his head and captured my bottom lip, gently sucking it into his mouth.

"Tell me you want this," he mumbled against my lips.

Did I want it? Yes, very much so. Was it a good idea? Probably not. I needed food and shelter far more than my desires needed to be sated, though it was beyond difficult to think logically with all that was Copper looming over me.

When I took too long to answer, he pulled back and met my eyes. "All you have to do is say no, and I'll leave," he said softly.

"And then what happens?" I whispered.

His brows furrowed and then realization

dawned. "Layla, this has nothing to do with providing for you for a few weeks. I was going to offer to help you out anyway, but Phoenix ordered it when he found out about you, and I'm happy to do it. There're absolutely no expectations of repayment in any form from you. Having said that, I've wanted you from the moment I laid eyes on you."

"I'm not a whore," I blurted.

"Never thought you were, Locks."

"I pretty much have to rely on you for everything right now, and I don't want to make things awkward between us."

He grinned and lowered his mouth to my neck. "Wasn't planning on this being a one-time thing, woman."

"Oh," was the only response my mind could conjure up.

He worked his way up to my ear, his warm breath tickling my skin when he spoke. "I need the words, Locks."

Fuck it. I deserved to have some fun. "Show me whatcha got, biker boy."

Those few words from me flipped a switch I didn't know existed. Copper rose up on his knees and ripped my shirt over my head as he went, leaving my braless breasts to bounce free. Next, he lost his shirt and shoved his jeans down his legs. Climbing onto the bed in his boxer briefs, he reached for the waistband of my pants and panties, removing them both in one fell swoop.

He fell on top of me and groaned. "Fuck, Layla. You're one sexy ass woman."

He covered my mouth with his and proceeded to devour me. Then, he slid down my body and captured my nipple between his teeth, alternating between sucking and gently biting. He moved and gave the other side the same treatment. By the time he released my breast, I was writhing on the bed and moaning like a shameless hussy.

"Copper," I breathed, tugging on his hair.

He chuckled against my stomach, but continued sliding down my body until his face was between my legs. I was incredibly uncomfortable with this turn of events. No man had ever put his face between my legs before, and to my utter horror, I heard him inhale deeply.

I tried to push him away, but the big bastard grabbed ahold of my thighs and held me in place while he extended his tongue and slowly licked me from bottom to top. He groaned loudly, and I forgot how to breathe.

Continuing with his ministrations, I gasped for air and got lost in the pleasure his mouth was providing. My eyes flew open when he pushed two fingers inside me and started sliding them in and out causing my body to curl up on its own volition as my mouth opened in a silent scream.

And that's when he curled those two fingers in a come-hither motion. My pussy clamped down on his fingers and pulsed with wave after wave of pleasure as I exploded into orgasmic ecstasy. "Copper," I moaned, trying once again to pull him closer by his hair.

He climbed up my body and took my mouth with his, not caring one bit that he was covered with my arousal. I could taste myself on his lips and tongue, and surprisingly, I liked it.

My thoughts were interrupted when Copper pulled away and met my eyes. "Condom?" I asked.

"Already on, Locks," he said right before he thrust his length inside my slick entrance and buried himself to the hilt in one fluid movement causing my body to slide from the force.

He let out a guttural groan but froze when I dug my nails into his back and used his shoulder to muffle the inhuman sound that bubbled up from deep within. "Locks?" he asked.

I could hear the worry in his voice, but I was too busy trying to breathe through the pain to answer him. When he started to pull out, I was quick to respond. "Don't move," I gasped and clung to his body.

"Layla, talk to me. What's wrong?"

How was I supposed to answer that when I didn't even know? I inhaled deeply and blew it out slowly. "M-my leg. The stitches are caught on something," I blurted.

He turned his head and looked down the length of our bodies. "Looks like it's the crocheted blanket under us. Let me ju—"

"No! Whenever you move, it pulls more."

"Fuck. Shit. Okay, um—"

"Drop your weight on me and push up on your toes. Then, roll when I do," I instructed.

He did what I asked without arguing. With his knees off the blanket, I was able to grab it while we rolled. Once I was sitting up, I quickly untangled the blanket from the line of stitches in my calf.

"Is your leg okay?" Copper asked.

"I think so. It's not bleeding, and it doesn't

look like any came out," I said and turned to look at him. The heat in his eyes was unmistakable.

"Good. Now get that fucking blanket off the bed so I can fuck you like I want to before you make me come by just sitting that hot pussy on my cock."

With a flick of my wrist, the blanket went sailing to the floor. Copper's knees came up, and his hands landed on my hips while he thrust upward. "Ride me, Locks."

I started to move, tentatively at first, but soon had a steady rhythm going. I was really getting into it and thought I might come again—which had never happened before—when Copper suddenly sat up and flipped me to my back, following me down.

"Couldn't take much more of you riding me looking like a fucking goddess," he said and started moving at a steady pace with nice, hard thrusts.

He hooked my uninjured leg with his arm and brought it up, so my knee was damn near touching my chest, allowing him to sink even deeper into me. "Reach down and rub your clit for me. I want to feel that pussy squeezing my cock harder than it squeezed my fingers," he ordered before sucking hard on my nipple.

"Copper," I gasped as I moved my hand between our bodies. "Oh, fuck, don't stop."

"Fuck, yes," he groaned and increased his pace. Half a dozen thrusts later, a second orgasm crashed through me moments before Copper found his own release.

He lowered his head and softly pressed his lips to mine. "Yeah," he said softly, "we're doing that again."

15

COPPER

A few days had passed since things came to a head with Layla. I was still waiting to hear back from Badger about Evelyn's whereabouts.

Even though I assured her the club would take care of her because she was family, she insisted upon earning her keep, as she put it. Much to my chagrin, I did need someone to fill in behind the bar since it was taking all hands on deck to work on the clubhouse repairs. When I asked her if she would be willing to fill in, she readily agreed and informed me she had worked part-time as a bartender prior to being kidnapped.

Since she was going to be working at the clubhouse and Leigh lived in the opposite direction from my place, I convinced Layla to stay with me. I didn't have anything fancy, but it was far from being a dump. Layla, however, acted like my house was comparable to an upscale penthouse. She also insisted on staying in a separate room. I didn't like it, but, ultimately, it didn't matter. I could fuck her in my room, the guest room, the kitchen, or wherever.

Being with Layla at night was the only thing keeping me from losing the last bits of my sanity. After a week of searching, we still had no idea who attacked the clubhouse. On top of that, Spazz hadn't been able to find much information on the new President of the Disciples of Death. I couldn't say I was surprised since we only knew the guy's road name. And no one was talking. Boar and I had both put feelers out. Both of us had a few guys making rounds at local bars listening for chatter, and both of us had come up empty-handed.

Layla's piercing scream had me on my feet and sprinting to the common room, as well as every brother in the general vicinity. Layla was standing on top of the bar, screaming the place down, but she froze when her eyes landed on all the guns pointed at her.

"Locks?" I questioned as I scanned the area for the threat.

She sniffled, and my eyes shot up to see tears streaming down her pale face as she pointed behind the bar with a shaky finger. "S-sn-snake," she stammered.

I sighed, partially in relief and partially in exasperation, and holstered my gun as I walked around behind the bar and scooped up Slither. "Sorry, Locks. They don't get out often, but when they do, they look for somewhere warm and below the ice machine is one of their favorite places."

"They?" she shrieked. "There's more?"

I chuckled, "Just one more. This is Slither, and the other one is Squeeze. Bronze and I got them for Christmas when we were kids. Will you hold him so I can see if Squeeze is under there, too?"

She was already shaking her head and holding her hands out to ward me off. "Hell, no. You and your snake stay away from me!"

"That's not what you said last night," I smirked and her cheeks flushed.

"Well, it's what I'll be saying tonight for damn sure," she said and planted her hands on her hips.

"I'll take him," Bronze said. "Sorry, bro, I guess I forgot to latch the top of their cage."

I rolled my eyes. "It's not the first time, and I'm sure it won't be the last."

He laughed. "Nothing will ever be as bad as the first time they escaped."

"What happened the first time?" Layla asked.

Bronze began telling her the story while I crawled around on the floor looking for the damn snake. "Like Copper said, we got them for Christmas when we were kids. We begged and begged for them for months, and finally, our dad got our mom to agree. We were so excited about them that I guess we forgot to latch the cage. Mom went to take a nap before dinner and found them curled up under the covers in her bed. Let's just say, after that, we didn't forget to latch the cage again until we were out on our own."

"Got him," I said proudly as I pulled the three-foot-long snake out from under one of the couches.

Layla shuddered. "I don't think I can work here any more," she whispered.

"Aw, Locks, they're harmless."

"Says the President of a motorcycle club.

Somehow, I think your definition of harmless has been skewed."

"That might be the case in some instances, but I'm serious, these guys won't hurt you. They're nonvenomous and too small to kill a human by constricting," I explained.

"They can still bite," she argued.

I nodded. "Yes, they can, but we've had them for over twenty years, and they've never bitten anyone. While they're pretty to look at, they're actually very boring pets."

A look of sudden horror washed over Layla's face. "Where do those things live?" she whispered.

"They've always lived at the clubhouse. After they got out on the first day, Mom wouldn't let us bring them home. Their habitat is in Spazz's room," Bronze said.

"Why Spazz's room?"

"They were in Bronze's room but had to be moved after the attack," I grumbled.

"Oh, well, at least they weren't hurt," Layla said awkwardly.

"Yeah," I replied and handed Squeeze to my brother. "Latch the cage this time, bro. I need to get back to work."

A few hours later, I was elbow deep in invoices

when someone knocked on the door. "Come in," I called out.

Tiny, my Road Captain, came through the door with a manila envelope in his hand. "A courier just delivered this at the gate," he said, placing it on my desk.

Assuming it was more paperwork for the damn insurance company, I ripped it open and pulled out the stack of papers. I was confused at first, unsure of what I was seeing. When it clicked, I closed my eyes, opened them, and looked at the papers again. Nope, they were still the same.

Jumping to my feet, I clutched the papers tightly in my hand and pushed past Tiny into the hall. "Church! Now!" I bellowed.

"Prez?" Tiny questioned.

"Not now. Round up the officers, quickly," I ordered, already heading to Church.

Not even five minutes later, every officer was seated at the table, all eyes focused on me. I held up the stack of papers. "These were delivered to the gate by a courier about ten minutes ago." I tossed the papers on the table for the boys to see, but continued talking. "It's a detailed list of every club member in the Devil Springs chapter. When I say detailed, I'm talking road name, full legal

TEAGAN BROOKS

name, date of birth, picture, address, names of family members."

"Do we know who sent it?" Bronze asked.

"I would guess the same fuckheads that destroyed part of our clubhouse last week. Other than that, no, I don't know who sent it."

Judge slammed his hand on the table and barked, "No one touch those papers. I'll bag them and check for prints when we're finished in here."

"Thanks, brother. The envelope is in my office on my desk. I thought it was more shit from the insurance company and tore right into it."

He shrugged, "Likely wouldn't get much off the envelope anyway. If it was delivered via courier, it's likely been handled by too many people to be of any help. Anyone else touch the papers besides you?"

I shook my head in answer, then said the word none of us wanted to hear. "Lockdown."

I dropped back into my chair at the head of the table and rested my head in my hands for a few brief seconds. "I want everyone listed in those papers inside the gates before dark. No exceptions. Follow the plan in place for notifications. Send prospects out to pick up family members if they can't or won't get here.

154

I'll work on the accommodations in the meantime."

With that, they dispersed and started notifying members and their families. I dreaded the next task on my to do list, but it had to be done. Picking up my phone, I tapped his name and waited.

"Phoenix Black."

"Just put my entire club on lockdown," I said wearily and proceeded to tell him about the envelope and its contents.

"I hate to say it, Copper, but there's not much more you can do at this point. Work on making arrangements and getting everyone secured. Let me know if Judge finds anything. Or if anything else happens. Stay safe, cousin."

"Thanks, Phoenix. I'll do my best," I replied.

"You always do. We'll talk soon."

I closed my eyes and tilted my head back. How was I going to find a place for everyone to sleep short of throwing sleeping bags on the floor and hoping people watched where they stepped? Our club wasn't huge, but we had a decent number of members. Counting their immediate family members, the number of people easily tripled what we could accommodate prior to the attack. Other than pitching tents behind the clubhouse, I had no idea what to do. Then, I realized tents wouldn't work because it was the end of February and way too cold.

Finally, it dawned on me. Bunk beds. The guys wouldn't like it. Hell, no one would like it, but it would work. If I filled the largest shed out back with bunk beds and put two sets in most of the rooms inside the clubhouse, we would have enough beds for everyone. Feeling better about the plan, I reached for my phone to get the ball rolling.

I was interrupted by yet another knock at the door. "Come in," I said distractedly.

Layla came through the door with a frightened look on her face. Once I took in her wide eyes and the way she was wringing her hands, I was on my feet and rounding the desk in an instant. Wrapping my arms around her, I asked, "Locks, what's wrong?"

She pushed against me and raised her head to meet my eyes. "You tell me. Why is everyone running around like some sort of apocalypse is approaching?"

I wasn't sure how she would handle it, but I decided to be completely honest with her. I told her about the delivery and all it entailed. Then, I explained how a lockdown at the clubhouse worked. The entire time I was talking, I was waiting for her to bolt, but she didn't. She listened to every word I said, and then she floored me with the next words out of her mouth.

With a furrowed brow and a wrinkled nose, she said, "I don't understand. If you think everyone listed is in danger, why would you lock them all in a place that has already been attacked? They could get everyone on that list in one go."

I had no words. She was right. Fuck! I was playing right into their hands. I cupped her cheeks and pressed my lips to hers. "Baby, I'll thank you later, but right now I've got to get busy. You, woman, may have just saved my whole damn club."

She looked shocked, but I had to turn away from her. I didn't want her to see the emotion I could feel welling up inside of me. I almost put all of my brothers and their families in a death trap. On the flip side, what in the hell was I going to do now?

I felt her small hand land on my back. "I'll be out at the bar. Let me know if I can do anything to help," she said softly before leaving the room.

Again, I turned to my older cousin for guidance. I was man enough to admit when I was in over my head and needed the help. I called and told him about the conversation I had with Layla. He was impressed by her observation and completely agreed. "I think I can help. Let me make a call, and I'll get back to you in a few. Sit tight."

The ten minutes it took for him to call back felt like ten hours. There was so much I needed to do, but I couldn't move forward without a plan, and said plan was in Phoenix's hands. I was never good at waiting or delegating. I was the kind of man who took charge and fixed the problem.

"I've got a secure location for you. You might not like it, but it is what it is. Boar has a rental house in Reedy Fork that's currently vacant and sits on a shit ton of land. The house itself is huge, but there's an even bigger house on the property that's completely hidden. As in, you have to take an ATV to get to it. Now, you're more than welcome to bring your club to Croftridge and stay on the farm, but I'm guessing you want to be closer to Devil Springs in order to get this sorted, right?"

"You've got that right. Plus, I don't want to

bring trouble your way, not when your girls are ready to pop, and you've finally managed to have a few months of peace."

"I appreciate that, but trouble looming or not, you and yours are always welcome here. Now, as far as Boar's place, he said you could start sending people to him right away. I would suggest having the families leave as discreetly as possible from their respective homes instead of coming to the clubhouse and leaving as a unit. You never know where they have eyes, and it's obvious they do have eyes on you."

"Good point. Thanks for your help, Phoenix. I'm in over my head with this one."

"That's what makes you a good leader; you can admit when you need help, and you don't hesitate to ask for it. You also took what Layla said seriously, even though she's new to you and the club. I'm proud of you. Now, enough of the sappy shit. Get done what needs doing and call if you need me."

Once again, I felt myself choking back my emotions. I didn't have time for that shit. Redirecting my focus, I spent the next few hours notifying everyone of the new plans. I was, of course, met with a variety of reactions, Leigh's being the most colorful.

"I'll cooperate with a smile on my face and keep all complaints to myself for the duration of our stay if you'll grant me one request," she said in an eerily sweet tone.

"And that would be?" I asked, dreading what I would hear next.

"I want you to put the whores at Boar's clubhouse. They have no business being around the families and potentially causing drama or scarring children with their late-night proclivities. A child doesn't need to learn what a threesome is when they wake up in the middle of the night wanting a drink of water. As an added bonus, you could tell Boar it's your way of thanking him for his hospitality. I mean, they're whores; whore them."

"If I do this, you'll willingly comply and hold all complaints?" I asked.

"You have my word. I'll even help out with the cooking and the cleaning," she offered.

"You've got a deal."

"Great!" I could hear the smile in her voice. "I'll head out soon and see if I can help Boar with the preparations."

"Actually, if you wouldn't mind, I'd like you to be in charge of the room assignments. You know the ins and outs of who should and shouldn't be roomed together, or near each other, or in the same damn house."

"I'll be happy to. See you tonight."

The rest of the day was complete and total chaos. I had to recharge my cell phone twice before I ever left the clubhouse. As if I didn't have enough to deal with, it started snowing around two o'clock. By the time Layla and I made it back to my place, packed our bags, and were ready to get on the road, there were several inches of snow on the ground, and it was dark.

"Are you sure this is a good idea? I'm thinking we should wait until morning to leave," Layla said as she peeked out the window at the still falling snow.

"We can't wait until morning. They're saying this storm is going to dump at least eight more inches over the next few hours. We won't be able to get there if we don't go tonight. It could be days before the roads are cleared."

"If that's the case, then isn't the same true for whoever is threatening the club? If we can't get through, neither can they."

"Maybe. Maybe not," I huffed. "I don't have time to argue with you about this. We need to get moving. Are you finished packing?"

She grumbled something I couldn't make out before saying, "Almost. I need to grab a few things from the bathroom, use the facilities, and then I'll be ready."

I finished packing and carried my bag out to the truck parked in my garage. I wasn't thrilled about driving to Reedy Fork in the midst of a snowstorm, but I was less thrilled about staying in my house with Layla like proverbial sitting ducks.

Turning to go back inside and hurry her along, I froze mid-step when I heard a noise I could only describe as one solid force crashing into another. It was unbearably loud and left no doubt in my mind that whatever it was had left destruction in its path. Then, everything went black.

16

LAYLA

I completely disagreed with Copper. I thought it was far too dangerous for us to drive to Reedy Fork. We would be fine until the storm let up and the roads were cleared. Then, I would be more than happy to go to Reedy Fork.

I was in the bathroom, hastily tossing my toiletries into a bag when I heard a loud crash, or maybe it was a crunch. I had no idea what it was, but it was alarmingly loud and had me damn near jumping out of my skin. Then, the freaking power went out leaving me in total darkness and an eerily loud silence.

I managed to feel my way along the wall and find the doorway. "Copper?" I called out.

When he didn't answer, my pulse ratcheted up a few notches. I crept further into the hall, keeping one hand on the wall to guide me. "Copper?" I called again.

I heard a door open and close followed by heavy footsteps. I froze and forced myself to breathe quietly.

"Layla?" Copper called, causing me to sag with relief.

"Copper, what happened?" I asked.

"I don't know. I came inside to find you first," he answered, his voice sounding closer.

"I'm in the hall outside of the bathroom."

"Stay there. I'm going to get a flashlight from my bedroom."

After several thuds, followed by cursing, he returned to the hallway with a flashlight. Correction, what he had in his hand could rival a stage spotlight. "Where did you get the mother of all flashlights?" I asked, genuinely curious.

He smirked, "It's a military grade tactical flashlight, the brightest one on the market."

"Of course, it is," I said flatly.

"Come on," he said, reaching to grab my hand. "Let's go see what that noise was?"

Noise? Sonic booms weren't as loud as

whatever just happened, but I chose to keep that opinion to myself as he was already dragging me along behind him. When we reached the living room, he handed me the beam of light and suddenly had a gun in his hand. "Keep the light pointed at the door, but stay behind me," he ordered and yanked open the front door.

"Fuck!" he cursed, lowering his gun and moving to the side so I could see. A large tree had crashed through his front porch, effectively blocking the front door. "I knew I should've had that damn thing cut down."

I laughed, "Looks like you don't have to worry about it anymore."

He gave me a flat look. "You do realize this means we're stuck here for the next few days at least, right?"

"Why is that?"

"Driveway's blocked," he said and pointed to the right. I stood on my tiptoes and followed his finger. The tree had fallen across his driveway and narrowly missed taking out his garage.

"I can think of worse things than being stuck in a house with you during a snowstorm…" I trailed off and gave him a coy look.

He closed the door and locked it. "Stay here

while I get a flashlight for you. Then, I need you to help me make sure all doors and windows are locked. We also need to shut all interior doors and close off the entry points to this room. Then, I'll get a fire started to keep us warm. Oh, can you grab blankets and pillows from the bedrooms?"

I couldn't contain the smile spreading across my face. I was stuck in a house with an incredibly sexy man, complete with little to no lighting and a fire. Oh, yes, I could work with that. "Of course, whatever you need," I said and placed a kiss on his cheek.

He returned with another flashlight on steroids and sent me on my way to complete my assigned tasks. It didn't take us long to secure the house and gather the necessary items. He got started on the fire while I used bed sheets to block off the open entryways to the room. Thankfully, there were only two I had to contend with.

I finished making us a cozy place to sleep before he was satisfied with the fire, so I snuck into the kitchen to grab something I saw earlier in the week. When I returned, he stood and turned to face me. I held the bag up and asked, "Please? I've never done it before."

He laughed, "You want to roast marshmallows in my fireplace?"

"I don't believe there's a stipulation requiring them to be roasted outside."

He grinned, "I suppose you're right. I'll be right back."

He returned with two wire coat hangers and set about straightening them. "Even though you've never done it, do you know how?"

I shrugged, "I guess so. Spear marshmallow, stick in fire, remove from fire, eat marshmallow, and repeat?"

He grinned with a mischievous twinkle in his eyes and handed me my coat hanger. "Have at it."

Not even two minutes later, I was shrieking, "Help! It's on fire. What do I do? What do I do?"

Copper was laughing so hard he was gasping for air and cradling his stomach. "Blow on it," he finally managed.

I rolled my eyes and did as he said. The flame went out, leaving me with a mass of charred goop. I glanced at Copper and saw a lightly browned, somewhat misshapen, marshmallow on the end of his coat hanger. "Dibs!" I declared and snatched his marshmallow, quickly popping it into my mouth, spawning an immediate mouthgasm.

Copper groaned. "You need to stop that," he said huskily.

"Stop what?"

"Making those sex noises while you eat."

I cocked my head to the side. "I never thought about it before, but it makes sense that orgasms and mouthgasms would elicit the same sounds."

"Mouthgasm?" he asked with a raised brow.

"Yeah. Like an orgasm in your mouth when you put something good in it," I said, not at all aware of how dirty it sounded.

"Oh, I've got something good to put in it. Come 'ere, Locks," he rumbled, and the air in the room suddenly charged with sexual energy.

I scooted over to where Copper was seated. When I was within arm's reach, he wrapped his hand around the back of my neck and pulled me to him. Leaning down so our noses were touching, his eyes flicked to mine before he captured my bottom lip and gently sucked it into his mouth.

I reached for his belt and started tugging at the buckle, but he grabbed my hand and stopped me. "I wasn't being serious, Locks."

I leaned back and looked at him with an arched brow. "Are you saying you don't want me to?"

"Oh, no, I fucking want you to; I just don't want you to think, I mean, I wasn't asking you to, uh, oh, holy fuck, Layla," he groaned as I took him into my mouth. While he'd been rambling, I'd been busy getting his pants undone.

I didn't have a lot of sexual experience, particularly with this specific activity, but from what I'd read in a few romance novels, as long as I didn't use my teeth, it would be enjoyable for him. However, I didn't want it to be just enjoyable; I wanted it to be fucking mind-blowing.

My movements were slow and tentative at first, but my confidence grew with each groan of pleasure from him. Before long, I was bobbing up and down on him in a steady rhythm with one hand working in time with my mouth and the other hand massaging his balls.

His hands landed on my shoulders, and he tried to push me away. "Locks, baby, you gotta stop."

My rhythm faltered for a moment when I glanced up to see his face. His jaw was tight and his eyes were squeezed shut. "Babe, I'm gonna come if you don't stop."

I wanted to say, "Well, duh, that's the point,"

but instead, I continued what I was doing and slightly increased my pace.

Copper's hands tangled into my hair, and he held me in place as he thrust his hips forward and filled my mouth with his release. I swallowed frantically, afraid it was going to start spewing out of my nose, and finally managed to get it all down.

Before I could register what was happening, I was on my back, my lower half was bare, and Copper's face was buried between my legs, and he was devouring me. His big arms were wrapped around my thighs to hold me in place as he did things with his tongue I didn't know were possible.

In an embarrassingly short amount of time, as in less than a minute, he had me orgasming against his lips. I assumed he would stop once the orgasm was over, but he didn't. No, not Copper Black. He changed to pulsating suction which had me curling into a half sit-up and reaching for his hair. He looked up at me with those intense blue eyes, and I could feel more than see the smug grin on his face.

"Oh, fuck, please," I panted.

He kept his eyes locked on mine as he released one thigh so that he could slide two fingers inside me. He winked, pressed his fingers against my g-spot, and I exploded into all-consuming, life-changing pleasure.

When I came back to reality, Copper was hovering over me with a pleased look on his face while my chest heaved over and over as I tried to catch my breath.

"You okay?" he asked with a grin.

"I, uh, yeah, I think so," I stammered.

"Good," he rumbled, "because now I'm going to fuck you." With that, he moved his hips forward and slowly entered me.

"Fuck, you feel good," I groaned.

"Shirt, Off," he grunted as he picked up his pace.

I quickly complied and ripped my shirt over my head before unclasping my bra and tossing it to the side.

"Love your tits, Locks," he murmured and buried his face between them.

I brought my legs up around his waist and clawed at his back, "More, I need more."

"Was trying to go slow," he said against my chest.

"No, Harder."

He pushed up onto his knees and hooked my

legs over his arms. Then, he leaned forward and planted his hands beside my head which damn near pressed my knees into my shoulders. He was so deep, and just when I thought he couldn't go any farther, he pulled back and gave it to me harder.

He continued thrusting into me, and just when I thought things couldn't get any better, he changed the angle of his hips so he was rubbing against my clit with every thrust and brought me to a third orgasm that bordered on painful. I screamed his name as I came, and he buried his face in my neck as he followed me over the edge.

"Fuck," he breathed against my skin.

"Wow," I whispered. "That was——"

"Yeah, Locks, it was."

After we cleaned up and got dressed, we cuddled together under the covers of our makeshift bed and listened to the sounds of the crackling fire.

"Whatever it is, go ahead and say it or ask it, Locks." I had been so lost in my thoughts, it's a wonder he couldn't actually hear them.

"How did you become the President of a motorcycle club? I know you said your cousin is also a President, so is this like a family thing?"

"It is. My grandfather, Talon Black, started the club with some of his friends when they retired from the military. He was the President for almost thirty-five years. When he died, my father, Hawk, took his place until he and my mom died in a motorcycle wreck five years later. At the time, I was too young to become President, so it was offered to Phoenix. A few years ago, Bronze and I were ready to get the Devil Springs Blackwings up and running again."

"What do you mean again? Was there one here before?" I asked.

"The original chapter my grandfather started was here in Devil Springs. Phoenix and his grandparents are from Croftridge. Shortly after Phoenix took over as Prez, his grandparents moved to Florida and left him their house and a lot of land. He proposed moving, the club voted, and that was that. Honestly, I think he did it that way so Bronze and me could have a chapter in the same clubhouse our grandfather and father once did," he said.

"He sounds like a pretty nice guy," I said.

"He is. He's been through more than his fair share of shit over the years, but he never gave up and managed to come out on top," he said proudly.

"How come you and Bronze don't have birdie names?" I asked, causing him to laugh.

"My mother, Goldie, was a bit of a free spirit. Some might even say she was a hippie or whatever. Anyway, she strongly believed in the natural healing powers of natural elements. She wanted to name her boys after precious metals and her girls after precious gems. She didn't have any girls, but that's how me and Bronze got our names," he explained.

"She sounds like an interesting woman," I mused.

"She was the best. Not a day goes by that I don't miss her," he said solemnly.

"Yeah, I know what you mean." And I did. My mother had only been gone for a few months, but I imagined that was a pain that would never go away.

He gently tightened his arms around me, as if he knew where my thoughts had gone. "If there's anything else you want to know, all you have to do is ask."

"Well, there is one other thing I've been curious about. Um, Leigh told me that you guys make your money legally, but what exactly is it that you do?"

"A lot of the members have their own jobs independent of the club, but, as of right now, the club owns seventeen rental properties, and we recently purchased a bar."

17

COPPER

L ayla fell asleep almost immediately after she cleaned up in the bathroom. I grabbed my phone from the coffee table and slipped out of the room to call Bronze.

He picked up on the second ring. "Hey, brother. I'm not going to make it there tonight," I said.

"Why not? Did something happen?" he asked.

"Yes, but nothing like what you're thinking. Layla and I were about to get on the road when the power went out and that damn tree in the front yard fell on my fucking house."

"Shit. Are you guys okay?"

"Yeah, we're fine. She was in the back bedroom, and I was in the garage loading up the truck when it happened. Anyway, I can't get out of my driveway until I get the tree moved."

"Right, and there's probably tons of trees down between here and there. We still have power here so I'll turn on the news and see what they're saying about road conditions and such."

"Thanks, man. Did everyone get there okay and get settled?"

"Yeah, everyone except you. Leigh did a great job with the room assignments. She put the families with children in the bigger house at the back of the property and put the couples and singles in the other house. But she sent the whores to the clubhouse," he said, sounding disappointed.

"Sorry, brother, it had to be done. Is there enough room for everyone?" I asked.

"Plenty. Both houses are huge, and some of his guys had campers they set up for us to use. I tagged one of those for you and Layla."

"Appreciate it. I'm going to check in with Judge and Spazz before I call it a night. Call if you need anything," I said.

"Will do. Night, brother."

I breathed a sigh of relief. Knowing my entire club was safe for the time being was a huge weight off my shoulders.

Next, I called Judge to see if he found anything new with the security footage or the hit list. Judge sighed into the phone, "Yes and no. I figured out why there was nothing on the security footage. Someone got into the system and replaced the live feed with a loop of footage showing no activity. I think I know how they did it, and I'm working on fixing that now. Unfortunately, there's no way for me to get the real footage back. I'm sorry, Prez."

"Nothing to be sorry for, brother. It is what it is. We haven't had a need to tighten or strengthen our security since I started the chapter. This came as a shock to all of us. It ain't you, so don't let your head go there. That's an order, brother."

"Easier said than done," he grumbled.

"What about the papers? Did you get anything from them?"

"Not really. I got a partial print from one of the last pages, but I don't think that's going to be much help. The only other thing that stands out is the order of the names. Wouldn't most people list the President and VP first, followed by the officers, then patched members, then prospects? This list is all jumbled up, and I don't know what to make of it."

"Talk to Bronze and Spazz about it. Spazz is observant, and Bronze is good at figuring out patterns and shit."

"Will do, Prez. Oh, one other thing. The pictures included with the names are recent, some as recent as last week. Having said that, I noticed there is one name missing from the list..." he trailed off.

"What do you mean? Who's missing?"

"Layla."

"Fuck!" I cursed. "You think it's as simple as they haven't spotted her yet? She hasn't been anywhere other than the clubhouse or my house, with the exception of Leigh's place once or twice."

"I honestly don't know. I just thought it was worth mentioning. Are you going to be here soon?"

"It was worth mentioning, and I'm glad you did. And, no, I'm not going to make it until the roads are cleared, probably a few days." I went on to tell him about the power outage and the tree falling on my house. We talked for a few more minutes before I placed a call to Spazz.

"Prez, I've been waiting for you to get here. I've got some info for you," Spazz said.

"I'm not going to be there for a few days, so go ahead with what you've got."

"It's not much, but it's a start. The new President of the Disciples of Death goes by Aim. Through none other than a popular social media site, I was able to track down his legal name, Amos Brown. Through less proper channels, I was able to get enough information to do a background search on him. Here's the thing, he has no history prior to a few months ago. I'm talking no bank accounts, no credit history, no previous address, not even a damn speeding ticket. I have a hard time believing a Disciple hasn't received a traffic violation at least once over the years."

"Yeah, I agree with you. So, what are you thinking?"

"His name isn't Amos Brown, or that's not the name he was born with. I'm not sure how he did it, but I have no doubt Amos Brown's identity was created to hide whoever Aim used to be. I'll keep digging. I still have a few tricks up my sleeve that may lead us in the right direction."

"Good work, brother. Let me know the minute you find something."

After ending the call with Spazz, I closed my

eyes and went over the facts in my head. One thing stood out above all others. We suspected the Disciples of Death and were looking into them as if they were the culprits, but, in all honesty, it very well may not be them behind the attack and the threat.

Sighing, I made my way back to the living room and climbed under the blankets with Layla. Regardless of who was behind it, there was nothing any of us could do for at least a few days. With that in mind, I decided to take the opportunity and get a good night's sleep next to a beautiful and intriguing woman.

18

LAYLA

The next morning, I woke feeling well rested despite having slept on the floor. I was also alone and, based on the cold sheets beside me, I had been for some time.

After making a dash to the bathroom and shivering through my morning ablutions, I went in search of Copper. I was beginning to get a little concerned when I couldn't find him anywhere in the house, and then I heard the distinct sound of a chainsaw being started.

I peeked through the blinds, and there was Copper, out front working on the fallen tree with a chainsaw. I couldn't let him do all the work while I stayed in the house and did absolutely nothing. No, I was going to go outside and help, but first, I was going to figure out how to make fireplace coffee.

Fireplace coffee turned out to be much easier to make than I had anticipated. He had individual coffee bags that worked just like tea bags. All I had to do was heat the water in a pot over the fire, pour the hot water into a mug, drop in a bag, and wah-lah! Fresh, hot coffee.

While the coffee was cooling to a drinkable temperature, I ran back to the room I was staying in, or keeping my stuff in, and dug out the items Leigh loaned me. She ignored my protests and insisted I needed a pair of leather pants, a leather jacket, gloves, and some riding boots. As luck would have it, we wore the same size shoes. She assured me she had several sets of leathers, and it was no hardship to loan a set to me. Despite my initial reluctance to accept her offer, I was suddenly grateful that I did.

Once I was dressed in my makeshift snow gear, I pulled on a Blackwings MC beanie I found in Copper's room, picked up the still steaming coffee mugs, and headed out the back door. I took a minute to enjoy the beauty of the freshly fallen snow, undisturbed by footprints and tire tracks, before making my way to the front of the house.

Copper didn't notice me right away, the sound of the chainsaw masking any sounds from my approach. I couldn't take my eyes off him. Captivated by his rugged handsomeness, I didn't notice he had stopped the chainsaw and was staring at me. "See something you like?" he asked with a slight smirk on his face.

I ignored his questions and stepped forward, extending one of the mugs to him. "I didn't think it would be wise to startle you with a chainsaw in your hand. I was waiting for you to stop or notice me so I could give you your coffee. I thought you might like something to warm you up," I rambled.

He took the mug of coffee and took a tentative sip. "Thanks," he said, lifting the coffee in a mock salute, "but the sight of you in those leathers was all it took to warm me up." His lips quirked up at the sides as he raked his eyes over me from head to toe. "Don't get me wrong, Locks, your ass looks fine as hell, but you didn't have to put on all that just to bring me a cup of coffee."

I rolled my eyes. "I came to help with the tree."

"I don't need any help. Go back inside," he ordered.

I was taken aback by his response. I didn't

know whether to stand my ground or stomp back inside. Why couldn't I help? Because I was a girl? Too fragile and delicate to handle a task deemed to be man's work? Suddenly, I was overcome with anger. Without giving it much thought, I reached down for a handful of snow, packed it into a ball, and launched it at Copper, smacking him right in the chest, causing his coffee to splash on his jacket and his hands.

His eyes shot to mine. "What the fuck, Layla?"

"What the fuck is right, Copper!" I yelled, pelting him with another snowball.

"Stop throwing snowballs at me. What in the hell is your problem?" he asked as he placed his mug of coffee on the ground.

"My problem is you telling me to go inside because I'm a weak little woman who couldn't possibly help with something as manly as cutting up and removing a fallen tree!" I screamed, followed by another two snowballs, both hitting their mark.

His face was getting red, and his fists were already balled at his sides. "I didn't say any of the shit you just spewed," he barked.

"You didn't have to," I shrieked, launching another ball of snow at him.

"That's it," he said through gritted teeth and started toward me.

My fight-or-flight response kicked in, opting for flight. I turned on my heel and took off running as fast as I could. Between the inches of snow on the ground and the restraints of the leather gear, I wasn't moving very fast, making it easy for Copper to catch up with me.

I could hear his labored breaths behind me as I rounded the back corner of the house. Just when I thought I was going to make it to the back door, he launched himself at me, taking us both down to the ground. He landed beside me and quickly moved so that he was hovering over me, holding my arms above my head.

He lowered his face, only inches from mine, and searched my eyes, for what, I don't know, but I saw it, the moment he made his decision. His mouth crashed into mine with a force sure to leave my lips swollen and bruised, and I couldn't have cared less.

His hands slid down my body until he had a thigh gripped in each hand. Wrapping my arms around his neck, I tried in vain to pull him closer to me. I felt his weight shift, and suddenly we were moving. I tried to pull away, but he squeezed my thighs and grunted his displeasure. Before I knew it, I was on my back on the living room floor in front of the fire, with Copper pressing down on top of me.

I was expecting him to be rough, maybe even forceful. What I was not expecting was the gentle way he removed my clothes or the tender way he caressed my body. He took my lips in a soft kiss as he slowly pushed himself inside me.

He cupped my cheeks with his hands and met my eyes as he began to move his hips in a hypnotic rhythm. His eyes never left mine as our bodies moved together in perfect harmony until we reached our climaxes together.

"I don't want anything to happen to you, Locks," he whispered.

"Okay," I whispered back and nodded once.

"It's safer for you inside," he said softly.

"Okay," I said and leaned up to kiss him. All sorts of emotions that I wasn't ready to deal with were bubbling up in my chest and kissing him seemed like the perfect distraction.

He broke the kiss far too soon for my liking. "I need to get back out there."

"Yeah, I guess you do."

"So, we're clear on why I don't want you

outside helping with the tree?" he asked, his blue eyes sparkling with mirth.

"Yes, we are. And I'm sorry for how I reacted. Just, after everything that's happened to me over the last few months—"

He interrupted me before I could finish, "It's okay, Locks. I get it. You don't have to explain yourself to me. For the record, I'm used to being in charge and barking out orders without being questioned. I'll try to remember to explain myself next time."

"Thanks, Copper," was all I managed to get out. My throat was clogged with emotions I was desperately trying to swallow. Copper was like no man I had ever encountered before. He seemed to genuinely care about my safety and well-being, but he also seemed to care about me as a person, about my thoughts and feelings. I had never experienced that from a man before, and while I liked it, it also scared the hell out of me.

"Hey, what's going through your head? I can practically see the wheels turning," he murmured.

I shook my head. It was too soon to talk about feelings with him. Hell, we hadn't even discussed whatever was or wasn't going on between us. I had no idea if he thought of us as a budding new relationship or fuck buddies. Because I didn't want to hear one of those options more than I wanted to hear the other, I hadn't brought it up to him.

Not to mention, my future didn't have any certainties. I was pretty sure the only reason I was still around was because my leg injury and its subsequent healing coincided with the attack on the clubhouse and the latest threat. I had finished the antibiotics and had my stitches removed the same morning the list of names was delivered to the clubhouse.

"It's nothing. I'm fine, really," I insisted.

He chuckled. "I may not know all the secrets to the fairer sex, but I do know when a woman says 'it's nothing' or 'I'm fine,' it is something, and she isn't fine. Talk to me," he said with a softness in his eyes I couldn't ignore.

I also couldn't face him while I spoke. I gently pushed against him so I could move to a sitting position and cast my eyes away from him. "I'm just worried about how things will play out for me when all of this is over."

"When what is over?" he snapped.

"When I meet Annabelle in a few weeks and

you don't have to babysit me anymore," I said, refusing to look at him.

"Is that what you think I'm doing?" he asked harshly. When I remained silent, he snapped, "Answer me, damn it!"

"It is what you're doing! Because I'm related to Annabelle, you're obligated to take care of me until I can become her problem," I hissed.

He grabbed my face with both hands and pulled us nose to nose. "Fuck, Layla. You have to know that's not what's happening here." He leaned back and searched my eyes. "You're afraid," he said, a statement, not a question. "You feel it; you're just scared to admit it."

"I'm not scared to admit it," I said and paused. "I'm scared to want it. If I've learned anything from my life, it's that once I think I have something in my grasp, it will get snatched away from me in the blink of an eye," I blurted. My hand immediately covered my mouth as I stared at him with wide eyes, not believing I just shared one of my darkest truths.

He reached for me, but I moved away. "No, please don't," I begged, shaking my head. "I gave up on hopes and dreams a long time ago. I won't knowingly set myself up for the pain of watching a dream shatter ever again."

"Locks, baby, look at me," he softly pleaded. When I met his eyes, the compassion I saw in his blue depths had me choking back a sob. "It's too late to try and protect your heart. The only thing you're doing now is denying it, and denial won't stop the pain, baby."

The dam broke. I launched myself into his arms and buried my face in his neck while I cried out years and years of heartaches, disappointments, and losses. He held me in his arms, gently rocking me, never uttering a word.

When my tears finally stopped and I regained some composure, he tightened his hold on me and said vehemently, "You are not an obligation to me. I want you here. I want to take care of you. Damn it, Locks, I just want you."

I looked up and met his eyes. "You've got me."

"You've got me, too," he rasped.

19

COPPER

The time Layla and I spent snowed in was exactly what I needed, what I was looking for when I went up to Badger's cabin almost two weeks ago. While I'm glad I went, because I wouldn't have found Layla if I didn't, I did need those few days of solitude. To have found that solitude in my own home with Layla endeared her to me that much more. And that terrified me.

My club was attacked and every single one of my members was threatened, as well as their families, by a source we'd yet to identify. If anyone figured out Layla was important to me, she would instantly become a target.

I knew I needed to tell her she was in danger

by being with me, but I didn't want to. I was afraid she would run. Considering her recent past, I couldn't fault her if she did. But I just got her, and she felt like the lifeline I needed. There was no way I could let her go.

Maybe I could keep her with me and keep her safe without having to tell her anything. Once we took out the threat, all would be right again. An idea began to form in my mind, and the more I thought about it, the more I was sure it would work.

She came around the corner with a shy smile on her face, almost looking embarrassed. "What's that look about?"

She shrugged and turned her head, but not before I saw her cheeks flush. "I've enjoyed the last few days here, and I guess I don't want to leave."

I closed the distance between us and pulled her into my arms. "I know, baby. I don't want to leave either, but we have to. The club has been at Boar's place for three days waiting on me to get there so we can make plans and get back to our normal lives."

"I know. I just liked having you all to myself."

I grinned, "That's because I kept you well

fucked. Don't worry, Locks, I plan to keep up the good work in Reedy Fork."

She scoffed, "I'm not even going to acknowledge that statement."

"Didn't we recently have a discussion about denial?"

"I'm not denying anything. I'm ignoring it. Big difference. Are you ready to go?"

I threw my head back and laughed. She was too cute sometimes. "Yeah, Locks, let's roll."

The drive to Reedy Fork took much longer than usual due to the vast amount of road closures, downed trees, and accidents. Judging by the amount of destruction I saw, it would be at least a few more days before power was restored to Devil Springs.

Hours later, when we finally made it to Boar's rental house, I was greeted like I'd just been released from prison. The boys were on the front porch cheering and clapping. When I got closer, I was bombarded with handshakes and back slaps.

"It's about time you showed up," my pain in the ass brother said.

"Fuck off, Bronze. I got here as soon as I could. In case you missed it, a huge ass tree fell on my house. It took almost two days to get it cut up and moved so I could use my driveway."

"I'm sure having fresh pussy available didn't speed things up any," he said while glaring at Layla.

I fisted his shirt and met him nose to nose. "The fuck is your problem?"

He tried to shove away from me, but my grip was not relenting. "It must be nice being the president. You get to stay home and play with new pussy all day while the rest of us are sent away to figure out how to handle your fucking problems!"

"My problems?! Last time I checked, this shit involved the whole club. I didn't realize we'd started singling people out in our *brotherhood*."

"That was back when you cared more about your brothers than a piece of gash."

"Call her gash or pussy again, and I'll put you on your ass," I gritted out.

Bronze smirked and cast his eyes toward Layla, "How many times have you been bought and sold, sweetheart?"

A sob burst from Layla's lips, and I snapped. I cocked my fist and launched it at his face, but it never made contact. Vice-like arms clamped around my shoulders and pulled me back. I fought hard against them to get to the dickhead being held back by Batta. Tiny stepped in front of me and placed his hands on my chest to help hold me back.

"Breathe, Prez. Something ain't right with him. I should've said something, but I was waiting for you to get here," Judge said low enough for only me and Tiny to hear. "I think it has something to do with his head injury. He's been having major mood swings, angers easily, and he keeps forgetting things."

As Judge spoke, he continued pulling me away from Bronze and away from the crowd. My eyes darted around frantically, "Where's Layla?"

"Mom's got her. They went inside."

When he deemed we were far enough away, he released me, and I whirled around to face him. "Did you talk to Splint about it?"

"In a roundabout way. I asked about the lasting effects of a concussion and asked him to keep an eye on Bronze and the girls for any signs of trouble. If you didn't come today, I was going to call and tell you. It seems to be getting worse, not better, and the last thing he needed was another blow to the head."

"Good looking out, brother. Can you find

Splint for me?" I pinched the bridge of my nose and took in a deep breath. "This is the last thing we need to deal with right now."

Judge squeezed my shoulder. "We'll get him sorted and get this other shit sorted."

Fuck me. I should have known something was wrong with him. Bronze had never come at me with such hostility before. Sure, we got into fights and scrabbles when we were younger, but that's to be expected from brothers, particularly brothers who are only seven months apart. Thanks to Mom's fertility and Bronze's premature birth, we grew up more like twins. We were even in the same grade throughout school.

"What's going on, Prez?" Splint asked as he approached me with Judge following behind.

"I need to talk to you about Bronze," I said warily. It felt wrong to talk to him about Bronze's behavior before I talked to Bronze himself, but it was clear he was in no frame of mind to rationally discuss my concerns. I told Splint about Judge's observations and about the encounter I just had with him. "What do you think we should do?"

"Honestly, Prez, this is out of my realm of knowledge. I agree that something isn't right with him, but I don't feel comfortable trying to take a guess as to what might be wrong. You could ask Patch," he offered.

"Good idea," I said and wasted no time making the call.

After I brought Patch up to speed and asked what we should do, his response was immediate and filled me with dread. "Get him to a hospital now, Copper. Right now! Don't wait for an ambulance. Get him and go. I'll call ahead and speak to one of the doctors working there tonight. Don't wait another second, Copper. Now."

"Got it. Thanks, Patch," I said and ran toward the house with Judge and Splint on my heels. I didn't have to tell them; they could clearly hear Patch screaming his orders into the phone.

"He may try to fight us. Protect his head and restrain him if you have to," I ordered.

"I'm going to get Tiny and Batta to help," Splint said and took off down a hallway.

Judge led me to the room Bronze had been staying in since they arrived. I didn't bother knocking before I flung the door open and let myself in.

Bronze was on his feet instantly. "The fuck are you doing?" he growled.

I held my hands up to show him I didn't come

to fight with him. "Bronze, I need you to listen to me, as my blood brother, my best friend, right now. The boys said you've been acting strange since the explosion, and I just witnessed it myself. I called Patch, and he said we need to get you to the hospital right now. He said there's a good chance something is wrong, and they can fix it if we get there before it's too late. Please don't fight me on this. Let me help you, little brother."

He stood unmoving for a few beats. Then, I saw a flicker of fear in his eyes before he masked it with a neutral look. He shrugged, "Fine, I'll go let the doctors have a looksee, but, for the record, I think this is a complete waste of time and money."

"If it is, I'll make it up to you, I promise. Let's go," I replied and left the room. Thankfully, he followed without protest.

We piled into my truck, and Judge drove us to the closest hospital. The ride was silent for the majority of the trip, but Bronze started talking when we were five minutes away. "I've been having headaches. Well, I've had a constant headache since the explosion, and it's been progressively getting worse. I thought it would go away over time." He sighed and rubbed his hand over the back of his neck. I knew by that action alone he had more to say. "I knew I was acting like an ass, but I couldn't stop it. The smallest things were setting me off. I would suddenly be consumed with rage, and when it was over, I couldn't remember why I was mad. Like with you this afternoon; I know we argued, and I was pissed at you, but I don't remember why." Then, he tore my heart out when he asked, "What's going to happen to me, Copper?"

"We're going to get you to the hospital, and we're going to find out what's wrong. Then, we're going to fix it," I assured him, even though I had no clue if my words were true.

When we arrived, we were taken back to a room immediately. Judge and I were told to wait in the exam room while Bronze was whisked away to have some kind of scan done. Before Bronze returned, Patch came barreling through the door followed by Phoenix.

"Where is he?" Patch asked as he tried to catch his breath.

"They took him for a brain scan about an hour ago," I replied, rising to my feet to greet them.

"Good. I'll go find out what's going on," Patch said and left the room.

"You should have called me," Phoenix grumbled.

"I'm sorry, Phoenix. Everything happened so fast, and I—"

"There's no need to apologize. Just know you can call me any time for any reason, especially for something like this. I know I wasn't around a lot when you two were growing up, but I'm here now, and I'm not going anywhere."

"Thanks, man. How'd you manage to get here so fast? The roads were a mess when Layla and I drove up from Devil Springs."

He chuckled, "Shaker used his family's name and money to have a helicopter fly us here. I don't know how he did it, but we landed on the hospital's launch pad and were escorted inside."

"Be sure to thank him for me. I hate that you had to leave Annabelle and Ember. How are they doing?"

He smiled like a proud peacock. "They're getting bigger by the day, but I will deny saying that if you repeat it. Dash is staying with them at my house until I get back." He snorted, "Annabelle told me she would shove her foot so far up my ass her toes would tickle my throat if I didn't get my ass up here to be with you and Bronze."

I laughed, "That sounds like her. Sounds like Layla, too. Fuck! Layla..." Caught up in the mess with Bronze, I had forgotten all about Layla.

"She's fine, Prez. She's with Mom, and she knows what's going on," Judge added, looking up from the phone in his hand. "She said to call her when you had a chance, but to let you know she's fine and she understands."

My lips involuntarily curled into a shy smile. That woman was something else. Phoenix elbowed me in the ribs, "You're always trying to be like me."

I shoved him back and chuckled. He was right. Growing up, I had a bad case of hero worship for Phoenix. He was my badass older cousin, and I wanted to be just like him. In some ways, I still did, but I would never tell him that.

Patch came through the door; the look on his face causing my gut to twist. "Copper, I need you to come with me. They're taking him straight to surgery. We can meet them outside the operating room so you can see him before they take him in. Sorry, Phoenix, I can only take one person back."

"Not a problem, man. Go. Tell him I'm here, and I love him," Phoenix said. "We'll be here when you get back."

Patch all but sprinted through the hospital, which alarmed me even more. He hadn't said what was wrong with Bronze. It had to be something with his head, which meant my brother was being rushed to emergency brain surgery. The thought nearly sent me to my knees. This couldn't be happening. Not now. Not to Bronze.

Patch skidded to a halt as a rapidly moving stretcher rounded the corner. White coats were flapping, machines beeping, voices shouting orders as they closed the distance between us. Patch leaned closer to me, "You'll have to make it quick."

They stopped in front of us, and I stepped closer, grabbing Bronze's hand. "I'll be here when you wake up, little brother. Phoenix is here, too. Told me to tell you he loves you." I took a deep breath and choked back the emotion clogging my throat. "I love you, brother."

I wasn't seeing the badass biker my brother had grown up to be. To me, he looked like the same scared little boy he was when he was being wheeled into the operating room to have his appendix removed many years ago. "Love you, too, Copper. And I'm sorry, for whatever we were arguing about. I'm sorry."

"It's okay, man. I know it wasn't you talking." I squeezed his hand, "Go get better. I'll see you soon." He squeezed my hand in return, and then he was gone.

"Come on, let's go back to the room, and I'll explain what we found on the scan," Patch said.

When we entered the exam room, I took a seat, and Patch delivered the news. "The scans showed a small, slow bleed in Bronze's brain. It's so small that it's barely visible even now. So, this isn't something that was missed or overlooked. Due to the size and location of the bleed, it will be a somewhat challenging procedure for the surgeon. That's the bad news. The good news is a small bleed means less damage to the brain and higher chances of a full recovery."

"What are the chances of, of him," I couldn't finish my question, couldn't bring myself to utter the words.

Patch seemed to understand without saying the rest. "There is a risk with every surgery. A lot of physicians will spout off percentages and statistical data regarding expected outcomes. I try to avoid doing that whenever possible, because I feel like it's pointless. We never know who's going to fall into the favorable percentage and who isn't. What I will tell you is he has a phenomenal surgeon operating on him, the team in there will do everything they can for him, and he has his age and health on his side. The rest is out of our hands."

"Thanks, Patch. I appreciate everything you're doing for him." I closed my eyes and tilted my head toward the ceiling. The next few hours were going to be some of the longest of my life.

20

LAYLA

I was sitting in Leigh's bedroom, trying not to drive myself crazy with worry when a knock on the door startled me. "It's just me. Can I come in?" Leigh called from the other side of the door.

"Of course, you can. This is your room," I reminded her. I was told a camper had been reserved for Copper and I to stay in, but Leigh thought it would be better for me to stay in the house until Copper returned. I completely agreed with her.

She entered with her phone to her ear. "Here she is," she said and handed the phone to me.

"Hello?"

Copper's tired voice filled my ear. "Locks, baby, you doing okay?"

"I'm fine. How's Bronze? How are you?" I asked.

"I need you to keep this to yourself, okay?" I readily agreed, and he continued. "They found a small bleed in his brain from the explosion. They took him right into surgery after they found it. He's in recovery now and should be going to a room soon. The doctor said everything went well with the surgery."

"You don't sound relieved in the slightest. What are you not telling me?"

He sighed, "He's not out of the woods yet. There's a chance his brain could start bleeding again, and he would have to go back to surgery if that happened. On top of that, we won't know if there's any permanent damage until he wakes up."

"Oh, baby, I wish I was there with you."

"I know you do, but it's safer for you to stay there. Judge, Phoenix, and Patch are here with me. I don't know how long they're staying, but I won't be back tonight. Not sure about tomorrow. Where are you staying?"

"I've been hanging out in Leigh's room. She

said there was a camper outside for you and I, but she thought it would be better if I stayed in the house until you were back."

"I would feel better if you were in the house, too. Tell you what, I'll have Judge stay in the camper, and you can stay in his room in the house tonight."

Despite my protests, he insisted and I relented. He had too much on his plate to be bothered with trivial issues. We spoke for a few more minutes before he had to go, promising to call with an update in a few hours.

I handed Leigh her phone. She smiled, "Come on, I bet you're hungry." I really wasn't, but it sounded like I couldn't refuse.

I followed her through the house to the kitchen. The house was surprisingly quiet and seemed relatively empty. I had expected to be bumping into people left and right.

When we entered the kitchen, three women I had never seen before were standing around an island, each holding a glass of wine and laughing. They paused when they noticed us.

"Girls, this is Layla. She's Copper's friend who will be staying here with us. Layla, these three nuts are married to club members. From left to right, Tiffany, Lauren, and Andrea," Leigh said. All eyes shot to me. I tried not to squirm or fidget while they silently appraised me. Leigh cleared her throat and said sternly, "Not that kind of friend."

The group collectively exhaled and smiled. Tiffany was the first to speak. "It's nice to meet you, Layla. Would you like a glass of wine?"

"Yes, please, if you don't mind," I said quickly, eliciting giggles from everyone.

"Sorry about our initial reaction. We don't associate with the whores. Leigh doesn't either. So, we weren't sure how to respond when she introduced you," Andrea said.

I shrugged, "You weren't the first to think that, and I'm sure you won't be the last. No harm done."

"Leigh, what are you over there doing?" Tiffany asked.

"Making something to munch on."

"Just toss a bag of popcorn in the microwave," she suggested.

"I wholeheartedly believe popcorn was created by the Devil himself, and I refuse to make it, let alone eat it," Leigh stated before joining us at the table with the tray of cheese, crackers, and fruit she put together. "Dig in. I need you to soak up some of the wine you've ingested. It's too early in the day to deal with your drunk asses," Leigh said jovially.

Lauren winked, "We'll slow down and give you time to catch up."

Leigh took a seat at the table and grabbed a glass of wine, "Well, in that case..." Laughter erupted around the table. It was obviously a well-practiced routine between the women.

We spent most of the day in the kitchen talking. By the time Leigh showed me to Judge's room, I had each of the women pegged. Tiffany was the polite one, Lauren was the wild one, and Andrea was the blunt one. Their personalities seemed to complement each other well, and I found myself slightly envious of their bond. Maybe one day I would be blessed with similar friendships.

After a quick shower, I crawled into bed. Drinking wine for the better part of the day left me feeling sluggish and sleepy, until a ringing phone from somewhere in the room scared the ever-loving shit out of me.

I sat up and immediately noticed the phone

on the nightstand. When I saw Copper's name on the screen, I couldn't answer it fast enough.

"How is he?" I said as soon as the call connected.

"He's doing okay, Locks. He's woken up a few times since the surgery. He seems to be the same as he was before the explosion." Copper chuckled, "He's pissed about his hair, though."

"I would be pissed too if half of my head was shaved," I said. Bronze had beautiful long hair—though, he probably wouldn't like me calling it beautiful. "When he gets home, I can fix it for him, if he wants. I'm thinking he could totally rock the shaved on one side, long on the other look."

"I'll tell him," he said softly. "He also asked me to apologize to you for him. He doesn't remember the argument with me and demanded I tell him about it. I did, and he said, 'You have to call her and tell her I'm sorry. Do whatever you have to do to express my profuse and sincerest apologies.'"

"All is forgiven. If he hadn't said those nasty things about me, his condition wouldn't have been brought to your attention until later. If him calling me a whore saved his life, I'm okay with that," I said honestly. I knew Bronze didn't mean it. Don't get me wrong, his words were painful to hear, especially in front of Leigh and the other club members, but I knew he wasn't speaking his true feelings about me.

"You're an incredible woman, Locks," he said.

"You're pretty incredible yourself, Copper."

After a few beats of silence, I added, "Enough of the sweet shit. I'm starting to feel the urge to vomit."

His booming laughter filled my ear. When he quieted down, I asked, "Whose phone did you call? I saw your name on the screen and answered without thinking about it."

"It's your phone. Judge didn't tell you?"

"No, I haven't seen him since he took you and Bronze to the hospital."

"He must've left it in the room when he was getting his stuff. I asked him to pick up a phone for you a few days ago. You would've gotten it sooner, but the snowstorm messed that up."

"Copper, I can't accept this. I'm sure it cost a fortune and—"

He cut me off, "You can and will accept it. I've already told you the club will take care of you, which includes your safety and that means you need to have a phone. I don't want to hear any more about it."

"Fine. Thank you for the phone," I said flatly.

"You can thank me when I get back," he said huskily.

After we ended the call, I stayed in the bed and tried to fall asleep for hours. I tossed and turned to no avail. In the early hours of the morning, I finally fell into a restless sleep filled with unpleasant dreams.

21

COPPER

Bronze's surgery was a success, and he only had to stay in the hospital for a few days. After giving it much thought, we decided it would be best for him to recover at Phoenix's place in Croftridge. Bronze wasn't happy about it, but he eventually agreed it was for the best.

My club had been at Boar's place for a little over a week. It was past time to take care of our problems and get back to Devil Springs. Even though Boar insisted we were welcome to stay as long as we needed, I still felt like I was a week behind thanks to the snowstorm and Bronze's delayed complication from the explosion. Just thinking about what could have happened to my brother because some stupid fucker bombed our clubhouse had me fuming.

Crammed into the detached garage on Boar's property, I called Church to order. "Brothers, we're not leaving this room until we have a plan in place. Blackwings don't run and hide; we face our problems and end our troubles." A chorus of grunted agreements sounded throughout the cramped space.

"Spazz, did you get anything else on Amos Brown?" I asked.

"No, Prez, not a fucking thing. Whoever wiped his identity did a damn good job. I did get some info on the new VP. He goes by Asp, but his real name is Donald Jensen. He's thirty years old and has been with the club since his early twenties. He's been arrested numerous times for a variety of crimes, including murder, but they've never been able to make anything stick. As far as family goes, parents are deceased, no wife, no children, two siblings, both are also deceased."

"His parents and his siblings are deceased? Was it an accident or did he kill them?" Judge asked.

"Parents died when he was a teenager; his father was stabbed in a bar fight, and his mother overdosed a few years later. From what I could find, the sister died in a fire last year, and the brother's body was found floating in the river nine days after the sister died," Spazz said.

"Names?" Batta gruffly asked.

"Parents were Gregory and Trina Jensen. Sister was Crysta Jensen and brother was Kevin Jensen."

I banged my fist on the table. "We need proof that these fuckers are the ones who attacked our club!"

"Sorry, Prez. That's all I've been able to get. I'll keep looking," Spazz said nervously.

"I think some of us need to go back to the clubhouse. They can't attack us if they don't know where we are, and we can't catch them if they're not doing anything," Tiny interjected.

"Good idea, Tiny. We'll leave the families here with the prospects and a handful of brothers while the rest of us return to Devil Springs. All in favor?"

The vote to return to the clubhouse was unanimous. We determined who would be staying with the women and children and decided to ride out first thing the following morning.

I didn't like the idea of leaving Layla behind, but I liked the thought of her getting hurt or killed even less. Hopefully, she would understand and not put up too much of a fuss about having to stay. She and Leigh had developed a friendship, and she seemed to get along with some of the other Old Ladies. She would be okay without me for a few days. Honestly, I wanted to send her to Croftridge with Bronze, but I couldn't do that without Annabelle finding out they're sisters which wasn't an option until the babies were born.

I dismissed Church and went in search of my girl. I hadn't been able to spend much time with her since we arrived and I was going to make up for it the moment I found her. As luck would have it, she was in the camper and had just stepped out of the shower when I walked in.

"Hey," she said shyly. "Give me just a minute to get dressed and I'll make us something for dinner."

"There's plenty of food at the main house," I said gruffly and followed her to the small bedroom.

"Copper," she gasped when I yanked the towel from her and pulled her body against mine.

"Been thinking about you all day," I murmured against the soft skin of her neck as my hands moved over the curves of her body.

When my hand reached the apex of her thighs, she dropped her head back and moaned. My fingers found her center wet and ready. "Seems like you were thinking about me, too," I mused.

"Mmmhmm," she agreed with a slight nod of her head.

"What were you thinking about?" I asked and reached to pull my wallet out of my jeans.

"This," she groaned. "You coming in here and fucking me."

"Yeah? Did you touch your pussy while you were thinking about me fucking you?" I asked while I made quick work of opening my pants and slicking a condom down my shaft.

"No," she breathed. "I wanted to, but I didn't."

"Good. Hands and knees, Locks," I said and gave her luscious ass a light slap.

She eagerly climbed onto the bed, and I was buried inside her seconds later. "Layla," I groaned and took a minute to just enjoy the feel of her body surrounding mine before I started to move.

By the time we were finished, I needed a shower and she needed another one. Needless to say, we never made it to the main house for dinner.

The next morning, she walked me to my truck to say goodbye. I pulled her against me and wrapped my arms around her. Then, I said fuck it and covered her mouth with mine in front of the whole damn club. I didn't know when I would see her again so this last kiss needed to tide me over for a while. The sounds of hoots and hollers caught my attention. Without breaking the kiss, I lifted my middle finger in the air and silenced the bunch of immature jackasses.

When I finally pulled away, Layla's cheeks were pink and her lips were swollen. I contemplated taking her back inside for another round before I left because I couldn't get enough of the woman.

She placed her hands on my chest and said, "I can't believe you did that. The women are going to be all up my ass once you leave. They thought we were only friends."

I made a snap decision in that moment. I can't

say the thought hadn't occurred to me before, because it had, but I hadn't given it any serious consideration. Still, I knew it was the right thing to do. Without warning Layla, I turned her in my arms to face the onlookers and announced, "She's my Old Lady. Show her the respect she deserves or you'll answer to me."

I heard Layla gasp as the boisterous bunch fell silent. Placing my lips against the shell of her ear, I whispered, "You know what that means?"

She nodded and turned to face me. "I do, I think. Do you mean it or did you do it to protect me?"

Holding her gaze, I answered honestly, "Both, Locks." She grinned. "Give me one for the road," I said, yanking her closer. The little vixen kissed the ever-loving shit out of me without an ounce of shame.

When we broke apart, her eyes were shining with unshed tears. "Stay safe, Copper."

Caressing her cheek, I told her, "I'll do my best. I'll call you tonight. Stay in the house, and stay out of trouble."

"Yes, sir," she said with a wink and gave me a salute before stepping away from my truck. With that, I pulled onto the road and led the caravan back to Devil Springs.

The drive back took a lot less time than it did when Layla and I made the trip there. The snow and ice had long since melted away and it looked like the majority of the fallen trees had been cleaned up.

Seeing the clubhouse when I pulled through the gates sent a flurry of mixed emotions through me. It was always good to be home, and the clubhouse was as much my home as my personal residence was. However, seeing the section that was bombed had me ready to explode with rage. I had to keep reminding myself it could have been worse. It could have been much worse.

"Prez!" Judge shouted. "You need to see this."

The hairs on the back of my neck stood up and a feeling of dread washed over me. I took quick strides to my brothers gathered by the front doors. "How did that get in here? We locked the gates before we left. And what about the fucking cameras? Did they miss this, too?!?" I roared.

We had surveillance cameras scattered around the property that were set up to notify us if and when any motion was detected while we were away. Judge assured me the cameras had been updated to the highest level of security in his reach. He even consulted with Spazz, Byte, and Shaker's girl, Keegan, to make sure the camera feed couldn't be hacked again.

Judge shook his head, "No way, Prez. My phone has been blowing up since we arrived because I haven't turned the motion notifications off yet. Hell, I got at least twenty alerts that were nothing more than a squirrel running through the lot while we were in Reedy Fork. I'll go on inside and start checking the feed."

"Hold up. We need to clear the building first. If someone got past the gates, they could've easily entered the building," I said.

We divided into groups and started clearing the clubhouse and surrounding buildings section by section. With each clear called out, a little bit of tension was relieved.

As soon as the last section was cleared, Judge took off for his room, assumedly to review the camera feeds. I returned to the front of the building and picked up the manila envelope with my name written across the front.

I took it to my office and dropped heavily into the chair behind my desk. I knew whatever was in the envelope was something I did not want to see. I also knew that I had to look. Pussyfooting around it wasn't going to do me any favors. Exhaling slowly, I ripped the fucker open and dumped the contents on my desk.

On top was a photo of a girl who looked vaguely familiar. Behind it was a photo of a young man I didn't recognize. The third photo I recognized immediately. Gnaw. What the fuck? I put it to the side and quickly looked through the rest of the contents—photos of Octavius, Scream, and Belch.

Behind the last photo, I found a handwritten note. "All dead. All killed by Blackwings. No more Disciples die by the hands of Blackwings. Now, Blackwings will die by the hands of the Disciples."

I carefully gathered the note and the pictures and stepped into the hall. "Church! Now!" I bellowed.

"We've got our proof, brothers," I said and tossed the envelope onto the table.

I gave them a few moments to pass the stack around and look through the pictures. "I'm sure you all know the Croftridge chapter is responsible for the deaths of Octavius and Gnaw. As for Scream and Belch, we were told Aim and Asp were responsible. Regardless, it wasn't anyone from Blackwings. Now, about the other two pictures. Any of you know who they are? The girl looked a little familiar, but I couldn't place her."

Judge straightened in his seat. "Isn't she one of the club whores from Croftridge? I can't remember the girl's name. She was always drooling over Phoenix, even after he found Annabelle."

Recognition dawned. "Yeah, I think you're right. I'll check with Phoenix. Okay, what about the guy?"

When no one recognized him, I figured it wouldn't hurt to ask Phoenix about both. I snapped a picture of their pictures and sent it to Phoenix in a text asking if he knew who they were. I didn't have a chance to utter a word before my phone was ringing in my hand.

"What's going on, Copper?" Phoenix asked, his voice full of concern.

I put my phone on speaker and placed it on the table. "We decided to come back to the clubhouse, just the brothers for now. Found an envelope by the front doors with pictures of Octavius, Gnaw, Scream, Belch, and the two I sent you. The note said all were killed by

Blackwings, and there would be no more Disciples killed by Blackwings because they were going to kill us first. I know about Octavius and Gnaw, but the other four have me stumped. I thought Aim and Asp killed Scream and Belch. How the fuck does that fall on the Blackwings?"

Phoenix cursed. "The girl was a club whore, but she was a mole for the Disciples. She's the one who helped Octavius escape. When we found Octavius and Gnaw in the warehouse, she was there, but she was already dead. One of them shot her in the head before we arrived. Her brother was a prospect for the Disciples, and he'd been trying to kidnap Annabelle and did help with kidnapping Nathan. I can't say for sure, but I bet the guy in the picture is her brother. Scream claimed he knew nothing about what Gnaw was up to and said he didn't want any trouble with my club. He took care of the prospect as a show of good faith, so to speak."

"Names?" Batta asked.

"The whore's name was Crystal, and her brother's name was Kevin. I think their last name was Jenkins or something like that."

"Fuck!" I roared.

"What?" Phoenix yelled.

"Jensen. Their last name was Jensen. They're Asp's brother and sister," I explained.

"This doesn't make any sense. Why would he come after you? Their deaths weren't on the Blackwings, but if he's trying to blame us, he should be coming at me and mine," Phoenix said.

"True, but what about Scream and Belch? Maybe they think we had something to do with their murders," I mused.

"Nah, I think their misplaced blame falls on me for Scream and Belch as well. Yes, we killed Gnaw, who was a Disciple, but Scream didn't give a shit about it. Then, Scream agreed to kill Kevin to keep the peace. I'm sure his VP backed him on those decisions. I'm guessing the club didn't back their Prez and VP, though."

"So, why the fuck are they coming after me?" I asked.

"My best guess, because you're closer," he said.

"Are you serious?"

"Yes. If he wants to take out Blackwings, as in all Blackwings, it would make sense for him to start with your club. It's closer, newer, and smaller. Even though he would be very, very wrong, he probably thinks the club is too new to be of any strength."

"Son of a bitch."

"Like I said, it's just a guess. Now that you know the Disciples are responsible, what are you going to do?" he asked.

"Not sure of the details, but we're going to put a stop to it. There's no way I'm letting them take out my club and come for yours," I said.

"Talk it out with your boys and let me know what you come up with. I'm going to send some brothers your way to help you get this sorted," Phoenix said.

"No way. We can handle this."

"I'm not asking, Copper. Consider it an official order. If we guessed correctly, in a way, this is my club's fault. I'm sending some men to help. Do whatever you see fit with them. They'll be up there tomorrow. We'll talk soon." He disconnected before I could respond.

"We'll wait until Phoenix's guys arrive to come up with a plan. In the meantime, I want eyes on the Disciples' Clubhouse. Judge, can you and a couple of brothers get some cameras up without being seen?"

Judge grinned, "Absolutely, Prez."

"Take two brothers with you and get started now. Everyone else, stay close and stay vigilant. These fuckers have been a few steps ahead and have gotten the drop on us a few times now. That won't happen again," I said and tapped the gavel on the table to dismiss Church.

22

COPPER

Phoenix's boys arrived the next morning. He sent Edge, Coal, Savior, and two prospects, Grady and Isaac. All of them were newer to the club. But from what I knew of the three patched members, they were valuable assets. I wasn't crazy about putting Coal in harm's way because he was family; but, I wouldn't disrespect him or his father by sending him back to Croftridge.

"How's your Mom doing?" I asked before I realized what I'd said. "I'm mean Annabelle. Shit. Sorry. I don't really know how you guys handle that situation," I said, stumbling over my words.

Coal laughed. "I call her 'Mom,' and I also

call Kathleen 'Mom.' It's different, but it works for us. Mom's doing fine, getting bigger every day. Dad's driving her crazy hovering around her like a helicopter. I hope she pops those babies out soon, or Dad isn't going to survive."

I chuckled, "I bet. How's Ember?"

He smiled, "She's good. She has her own helicopter, but she's handling the hovering better than Mom."

I shook my head. "I can't believe they're having babies at the same time."

"Yeah, we definitely qualify to be guests on a talk show. Anyway, when you have some time, I was wondering if I could talk to you about something," he said, suddenly sounding nervous.

"Of course. I have time now. We can talk in my office," I said and started walking in that direction.

Once inside, I closed the door and gestured for him to have a seat. Dropping into the chair behind my desk, I steepled my fingers in front of me and met his eyes. "What's going on, Coal?"

"I was wondering how one would go about transferring chapters."

Of all the things he could have said or asked, I

was not expecting it to be that. "You want to leave your Dad's club?"

He looked down at his hands fisted in his lap. "I love my Dad, and I love the club. I'm just having a hard time finding my place in Croftridge. Ember has the farm and is starting a family with Dash. Dad has the club and Mom and the babies. And I, well, after everything that's happened in the last two years, I feel like I need to find out who I am. I don't want to be just Phoenix's son or just Ember's twin. I need to be me, and I can't do that until I figure out who I am, and that can't happen in Croftridge."

I exhaled a long, slow breath. "I have no problem with you transferring to Devil Springs if that's what you want, but you have to talk to your Dad first. The usual protocol is for the member to approach their president first. Once it has been approved, then you would ask the other president for permission to transfer. But I understand why you came to me before going to him. Make sure it's okay with Phoenix, and then come talk to me."

His relief was evident. "Thanks, Copper. I'll talk to him as soon as I get back to Croftridge."

"Good. Come on. We've got Church in a few minutes."

Once everyone was seated around the table, I called the meeting to order and introduced the members from Croftridge. "Have we gotten anything from the cameras on the Disciples' clubhouse?"

"No, not yet. But I do know how they got the envelope past the gates," Judge said. "They used a drone to fly it over the gates and drop it at the door."

"A drone? How fucking fancy. All right, boys, we need to come up with a plan to take these fuckers down. I'm open for suggestions," I said.

"I say we bomb their clubhouse like they did ours," Batta offered.

"I say we position ourselves around the clubhouse and pick them off with sniper rifles one at a time," Tiny suggested.

"I think we should start with grabbing a few of their boys and interrogating them," Judge said.

"We should intercept their next shipment and let them know we have it. We can tell them we'll return it after having a sit-down with Aim and Asp, only Aim and Asp, on our territory. If they refuse, we can threaten to turn the shipment over to Luke," Coal said.

"If we do that, the other members will likely be hovering nearby, ready to defend their President and VP, meaning the clubhouse will be empty. We can sneak in and plant a bug, a bomb, or whatever the fuck we want," Savior added.

I leaned back in my chair, rubbing my chin with my thumb and forefinger as I appraised the young Croftridge members. "I kind of like that suggestion. Brothers?"

Judge shrugged, "It could work. Do we know when their next shipment is due?"

"No, but I know who to ask if we want to go that route," I said.

After more discussion, we decided to go with Coal's suggestion if we could intercept the shipment in the next few days. I stepped out of the room and placed the call.

"Boar, do you know when the Disciples are expecting their next shipment?"

He chuckled, "Yeah, the stupid fucks have been doing their business like clockwork for the last two years. I can't believe they haven't been busted yet. Three days from now, it will be coming to their warehouse mid-afternoon," he said.

"Perfect. Can you send me the location of their warehouse?"

"I'll do you one better. I'll get you the warehouse and the last leg of the incoming route," he offered.

"Appreciate it, man. Everything still quiet in your area?" I asked.

"So far so good. I have a few boys ride by my hot spots a couple of times a day to make sure everything is as it should be," he said, letting me know he was keeping extra eyes on our people still in his rental houses.

"I can't thank you enough for your hospitality. I hope to have this mess cleaned up by the end of next week."

"Not a problem. Take your time, Copper. It's not inconveniencing me in the slightest, and Shannon is having a great time hanging out with the Old Ladies."

We ended the call, and I went back into Church to update my brothers. Boar sent the location and route immediately. It didn't take long for us to hammer out a plan. Once that was settled, all we had to do was wait.

Usually, three days isn't a long time. The three days we had to wait for the Disciples' shipment felt more like three years. We managed to make a huge dent in the repairs to the clubhouse during the days. Each night, I spent hours locked in my room talking to Layla. I missed her more than I ever thought possible. She assured me she was fine and had been having a good time with the girls, but I could tell she was saying it for my benefit.

When the day finally arrived, we rode to the designated location and patiently waited for the truck to make an appearance. I was a little on edge because I didn't know exactly what was in the shipment. I was expecting it to be guns or drugs, but it could be anything from stolen goods to a truck load of women. And it better not be fucking women. I wouldn't be able to contain myself if it was.

An elbow to my side had my head shooting up. Judge whispered, "There it is."

In the distance, I could see a box truck approaching us. I whistled once and said, "It's go time, boys."

Surprisingly, we were able to take the

shipment without any hassle. The driver had no idea what he was delivering, or so he claimed, and wanted nothing more than to escape with his life. We let him go once he had been properly threatened and drove the truck back to Devil Springs. Batta, Judge, and Tiny were like giddy little school boys who had just raided the candy shop.

Thankfully, an inspection of the shipment revealed that it was indeed guns they were expecting. They were shitty guns, but at least we didn't inadvertently get involved in the world of human trafficking.

"Good work, brothers. Let's give them time to realize their shipment is missing and start looking for it. We'll have Church tonight, and I'll make the call to Aim," I announced.

JUDGE AND I HAD BEEN WATCHING THE LIVE FEED of the Disciples' clubhouse for the better part of the evening. Needless to say, there was a lot of activity. I couldn't stop myself from laughing every time one of the Disciples frantically ran out of the clubhouse and took off on their bike. No doubt Aim was losing his shit trying to find their missing guns. I was tempted to wait until morning to make the call.

With my brothers gathered around the table, I dialed the number Spazz had located for Aim and placed my phone on speaker. He answered before the end of the first ring, "Aim."

"Copper Black," I said, trying to hold back my laughter.

"You motherfucker!" Aim screamed.

"Excuse me?" I asked, feigning innocence.

"You and your club stole our damn guns. That was a big fucking mistake, Copper. One I'll make sure you regret."

"I see. I guess this means you don't want the information I have for you. Oh well..." I trailed off.

"What information?"

"The kind that doesn't need to be discussed over the phone. You and Asp be at the old dive bar on Neely Ferry Road at ten o'clock tomorrow morning. Only you and Asp," I demanded.

"And if I don't show?" he asked.

"Then the info I have will be given to more *legit* sources."

"Fine," he huffed. "We'll be there."

"Oh, one more thing. If anything happens to me or any of my boys, the info goes straight to the feds," I said and disconnected the call. Now, we just had to wait.

23

LAYLA

I was starting to get a little cabin fever. I needed to get out of the house, even if it was just for a brief amount of time. And, I wanted to have a few minutes alone. I wasn't used to being around people every second of every day, and it was slowly driving me insane.

And I missed Copper. A lot. He called every night and sometimes we talked for hours, but it wasn't the same as being with him. I wanted to feel his arms around me, inhale his scent, have his lips pressed against mine. I wasn't sure how much longer I could stand being cooped up in the house away from him.

He told me not to leave the house. So, technically, the front porch and back deck were a part of the house. At least two men had been posted on the front porch at all times since Copper and the majority of the club returned to Devil Springs. That left the back deck. Surely, I could slip out there unnoticed and have a few minutes of peace to gather my sanity.

I tiptoed down the hall to the kitchen. It was late, and I was pretty sure everyone was asleep, with the exception of the two guys out front. I peeked through the window, and, when I was sure the coast was clear, I carefully pulled the backdoor open and stepped outside for the first time since Copper left.

Inhaling a lungful of cool, crisp air, I sighed. If only I had thought to bring a steaming mug of hot chocolate with me. Maybe next time. Curling up in one of the chairs, I tilted my head back and gazed at the stars. Before I knew it, I drifted off to sleep.

When I woke, my head was pounding, and I thought I was going to vomit. Deciding it would be best to be in the bathroom if I did indeed throw up, I moved to get out of bed. A cold feeling of dread washed over me when something prevented me from rolling my body to the side.

My eyes shot open and darted around the

room. Despite the darkness, I could instantly see I was not in any room I had ever seen before. I tried again to move and discovered my arms were restrained above my head. I tried my feet, and, thankfully, my legs were not restrained.

Forcing myself to remain as calm as possible, I tried to remember what happened. I was outside on the deck looking at the stars, and I fell asleep. Then, I woke up tied to a strange bed. What the hell?

With tears running down my face, I could do nothing but wait for someone to come in and pray they wouldn't hurt me.

It felt like hours of maddening silence passed before I heard a noise beyond the closed door, and the war within myself began. Did I want someone to come in, or did I want to continue suffering in silence?

I listened intently but heard nothing but silence. I'd almost convinced myself I'd imagined the sound when I heard someone wiggling the door knob. Moments later, the door flew open, and I immediately recognized the man filling the doorway. I could do nothing but stare at him as the tears poured down my face.

24

COPPER

We arrived at the bar thirty minutes earlier than we told Aim and Asp to be there. I wanted to make sure they weren't going to try something stupid like ambushing us when we walked in. The owner wasn't happy about having to open his doors to us at the early hour, but he owed me more than one favor and couldn't refuse my request.

I still wasn't one hundred percent sure how I was going to handle the situation. I had their stash of guns hidden, and a few of my brothers were guarding it. We had the two prospects from Croftridge monitoring the surrounding area for any signs of the Disciples. I had no doubt the rest of the club would be somewhere in the vicinity.

Tiny, Spazz, Coal, Edge, and Savior had ridden out to the Disciples' clubhouse to hopefully plant some listening equipment in their clubhouse. However, that might be a moot point depending on the outcome of the meeting.

Tension surrounded us as we waited for Aim and Asp to arrive. My phone chimed with an incoming text.

Grady: 15 Disciples pulled off into an empty parking lot app 1 mile from the bar. 2 riders headed your way.

Me: Thx. Text Judge ASAP if any of them leave.

Grady: Will do.

Minutes later, the two cocksuckers strolled into the bar, looking far too sure of themselves for my liking. They approached the table and dropped into chairs across from me with smug smiles on their faces. The taller one spoke, "In case you didn't know, I'm Aim." He gestured with his thumb to the man beside him, "And this here is Asp."

I nodded. "I'll forgo the introductions since you've made it clear you know everyone in my club."

"And then some," Asp grinned.

He was trying to goad me. I knew it, but damn if it wasn't working. I clenched my fists into tight balls under the table and resisted the strong urge to smash his fucking face in.

"Let's cut the shit and get to the point. What 'information' do you have?" Aim asked.

I shrugged, "Information about your shipment's location."

His jaw clenched and his whole body tensed. His VP, however, sat relaxed as the corners of his mouth turned up in an evil smile. "I see. As luck would have it, I've got some information about the location of something that might be of interest to you as well."

My heart skipped a beat, and my mind raced to figure out what he could have taken from my club. As if on cue, Judge's phone started ringing. He denied the call, but it started ringing immediately again. By the third time, he leaned in and whispered, "It's Mom. I've got to take it."

He stepped away from the table and answered the call. Even several feet away, I could hear Leigh screaming into the phone, but I couldn't make out what she was saying. Judge whirled around and locked eyes with me. All the color drained from his face while he listened to his mother. "Mom, I have to go. It'll be okay, I promise." She screeched something into the phone, and Judge cringed. "Mom, we're handling it now. I've got to go."

His words sent chills running down my spine. What had these fuckers done that would have Leigh calling in hysterics? Judge cut his eyes to Batta and gave the slightest of nods before meeting my gaze again. Were they waiting for something? Then, it hit me like a ton of bricks.

Layla.

Everything happened at once. Judge and Batta moved toward the table. My chair hit the floor when I pushed back and jumped to my feet. Judge had Asp on his feet and his Bowie pressed to his throat. Batta had a garrote wrapped around Aim's neck. I had a gun in each hand, one pointed at each asshole.

"Where is she?" I demanded.

Aim seemed to be genuinely confused, while Asp still had a cocky grin on his face. "Where's our shipment?" Asp asked with an arched brow.

I clicked the safety off on the gun trained on Asp. "Tsk, tsk, Copper. You should always think before you shoot. We also have backup plans in place. If anything happens to either one of us, she dies."

Aim's eyes cut to Asp as best they could given his current predicament. "What did you do?" he hissed.

"I did what needed to be done. If I hadn't, do you really think we'd have walked out of here today with our guns like nothing fucking happened? No, we sure as shit wouldn't have. It's war, man. Quit being such a pussy."

Aim squeezed his eyes shut and grimaced. I made eye contact with Judge and jerked my chin. Then, I did the same with Batta, only jerking my chin in the opposite direction. We were going to separate the two fuckers. I doubted we would get anything from Asp, but I had a feeling we could get something out of Aim. Regardless, neither one of them was going anywhere until my Old Lady was standing in front of me, and maybe not even then.

25

COAL

W e watched from afar as the Disciples pulled out of their forecourt—all of the Disciples. Seriously, they were morons. They probably assumed all of the Blackwings would be lurking around the bar in case the meeting got out of control. Little did they know, Copper had members from Croftridge lending a helping hand.

We waited for twenty minutes to make sure no one was coming back before we got to work. Using bolt cutters, we removed the lock and chain from the front gates. Spazz hacked their cameras and covered our activity with a loop of prerecorded video, just like they had done to Copper. Again, morons.

When Tiny turned the door knob and pushed the front door open, it was almost impossible to contain my laughter. "Stupid fuckers," he whispered. "Spazz, you, Edge, and Savior get started. Coal and I will watch your backs and make sure the clubhouse is clear."

Tiny pointed at me and nodded toward a hall. With my gun held firmly in front of me, I started moving down the hallway. It was lined with doors on each side and one door at the end. I was guessing it was the bedrooms of the patched members.

The first door I came to was wide open and confirmed my assumption. It was a bedroom, a thankfully empty bedroom. The door opposite it was closed. I pressed my ear against the cheap wood and listened for any sound. When I didn't hear anything, I carefully turned the doorknob and eased it open to find another empty bedroom.

I made my way down the hall, clearing one room at a time. When I was down to the last few rooms, I noticed names on the doors. Holy shit! How dumb could they be? Not only were the officers' bedrooms labeled, they were all together at the end of one hall. Anyone could take out all the officers in one go if they struck in the right spot, which is probably what they were trying to do when they bombed Copper's clubhouse.

I turned to clear the Road Captain's room when a noise had me freezing in place. I held my breath and slowly turned my body toward the direction of the sound. Staying as still as my frantically beating heart would allow me, I listened closely. After seconds that felt like hours, I heard it again, and it was coming from the President's room.

Creeping closer to the closed door, I silently waited. It sounded like the rustling of clothing and a faint squeak. It was probably just a rat judging by the condition of the place. The Disciples were disgusting fuckers. Just as I was about to turn back to the Road Captain's room, I heard another noise that had goosebumps breaking out over my skin.

I heard a moan, or maybe it was a sob. It didn't matter; it was decidedly human. Fuck! I kept my gun trained on the door and walked backwards down the hallway. When I made it to the common room, I whisper-yelled, "Tiny!"

He appeared seconds later from another hallway. I motioned with my gun, "There's someone in Aim's room."

"You sure?" he whispered.

"No doubt, brother."

"Let's go check it out. We know it's not Aim or Asp. Probably a club whore left over from last night."

We quietly, but quickly, made our way back to Aim's room. Tiny motioned for me to try the door. This time, the door was locked and, judging by the look on Tiny's face, that wasn't a good thing.

I reached into my pocket and pulled out my lock picking set. I wasn't as good as Edge, and none of us were as good as Reese, but I could handle a basic bedroom door lock. I would never admit it, but it took me a little longer than usual because my hands were shaking. I wasn't scared, per se, but not knowing what was on the other side of the door had me on high alert. I had no interest in being shot again.

Tiny counted to three with his fingers. On three, I pushed the door open and dropped to one knee. Tiny stepped forward with his hand cannon leading the way. "Fuck!" he roared and ran to the bed. "Shit! Are you okay? We'll get you out of here. Oh, fucking hell," Tiny continued to ramble.

I stepped up beside him to see what was going on. There was a woman chained to the bed by her wrists. She had a gag in her mouth and was only wearing her bra and panties. After scanning her for any possible weapons or injuries, my eyes landed on her face and everything stopped.

She looked like my mother, my biological mother. Her hair was covering part of her face, and the eye I could see was swollen and bruised, but there was no mistaking the resemblance. Hell, she looked like me and Ember. If it weren't for her flat stomach, I might have initially thought it was Mom or Ember.

With a shaking finger, I pointed to the woman and asked, "Who is she?"

Tiny was at the head of the bed working on the chains securing her to the headboard. I hadn't noticed Spazz or the other men enter the room, so I startled when Spazz spoke from behind me. "She's Copper's Old Lady. You boys head to the front and keep watch while we get her free. As soon as those chains are off, we're getting her the hell out of here. We'll call Copper once we have her somewhere safe."

I stood frozen, unable to take my eyes off the woman's face. "Why does she look like my mother?" I demanded. "Why does she look like me and Ember?"

"Because she's your mother's sister! No time for explanations. Now, go do as you were told," Tiny barked in a tone that brooked no argument.

I started to leave the room as I was told, but stopped to pull off my cut and then my t-shirt. I tossed it to Spazz and nodded toward the woman, "For her."

With that, I left and went to the common room with the other guys. My mother's sister? My mom didn't have any siblings. At least, that's what she told us. Why wouldn't she tell us about her sister? Especially with her being Copper's Old Lady. Nothing made any sense.

"Let's go, brothers," Tiny shouted as he came barreling toward us with the woman cradled in his arms.

"Give me the keys," I said to Edge. He handed over the keys to the cage without so much as a sideways glance. I ran ahead to the cage hidden up the road, climbed inside, and circled back to pick them up. They piled in and I sped off to the bikes.

Tiny waited until everyone was out of the cage except for the woman and me. He cleared his throat, "Coal, this is your aunt, Layla. Layla, this is your nephew, Coal. He's Annabelle's oldest son and Ember's twin. You okay riding with him back to the clubhouse?"

She nodded and softly said, "Yes. I'm fine as long as you're taking me to Copper."

Tiny nodded and focused on me, "Keep your phone handy. I have no doubt Prez will be calling as soon as I tell him."

With that, he closed the door, and we were on our way back to Devil Springs. And I had a shitload of questions to be answered when we got there.

26

COPPER

"Look, man, I know I owe you a few favors and all, but I can't have bloodshed in my bar," Henry said nervously. I swung my furious eyes to his. "I, I, uh, there's a storage shed out back you could use."

I nodded. "We'll start with Aim. Batta, you're with me. Judge, keep Asp locked down. The rest of you wait here and keep your eyes open in case their boys show up."

Batta and I moved Aim to the storage shed and prepared for a difficult interrogation. I was surprised, and slightly disappointed, when he cooperated with us and answered our questions. One look at the expression on Batta's face let me know he was equally disappointed.

I decided to start with the most important question, "Where's my Old Lady?"

"I swear I don't know. I know you have no reason to believe me, but I honestly have no idea what kind of shit Asp is trying to pull right now."

"Are you saying you didn't know he was going after my Old Lady?"

"That's exactly what I'm saying. Asp has developed a bad habit of making his own decisions, acting on them, and informing me after the fact. Up until now, it hasn't caused the club any trouble."

"Trouble isn't the only thing your club will need to worry about if anything happens to my woman," I spat. "Where would he have taken her?"

Aim exhaled, "Probably the clubhouse."

"And you expect us to believe she's at your clubhouse and you knew nothing about it?" Batta asked incredulously.

"I haven't stayed there the last couple of nights. I didn't go inside before we rode out this morning," he said and looked to the floor. Shaking his head, he added, "I should've been keeping closer tabs on him. What the fuck else has he done that I don't know about?"

"Anybody at your clubhouse who can see if my girl is there right now?"

He grimaced, clearly not wanting to answer, "Clubhouse is empty."

I jerked my chin at Batta. He nodded and stepped out of the storage shed. Hopefully, my brothers were still in or near their clubhouse and could look for Layla. So help me, if they hurt her, they were going to feel the same pain. Tenfold.

I continued with my questions while I waited for Batta to return. "Why are you after my club?"

He cleared his throat and kept his eyes on the floor, "I'm not after your club. Like I said, Asp has been somewhat of a loose cannon. I found out about the attack on your clubhouse after the fact. He argued his point, and I understood where he was coming from, but I would've handled the situation differently. If it's any consolation, he took an ass beating and was locked up for two weeks after I found out."

"It's really not. My brother, my blood brother, who is also my VP, almost died because of that shit."

"Fuck!" he cursed.

"Explain the pictures to me," I ordered.

His head shot up, "What pictures?"

I wasn't sure what to make of his response. Was he asking me to clarify which set of pictures I was referring to? Or did he even know about the pictures? "I received an envelope containing pictures of six people and a note claiming the Blackwings were responsible for their deaths and promising retribution."

His eyes widened and he cursed under his breath. "Who were the six people?"

I arched a brow. "Want to take a guess?"

"No, because it's not going to help my case when I tell you I didn't know about this either, especially when I get it right. Asp has been going on and on about retaliation for months." He straightened in his chair and pinned me with his eyes, "If you boys don't kill him, I swear I will if I make it out of here alive."

I didn't see that coming. "Let's not get ahead of ourselves. Back to the names."

"If Asp was behind it, and I'm sure he was, the pictures would have been of Scream, Belch, Gnaw, Octavius, Crysta, and Kevin."

I nodded. "Care to tell me why he thinks the Blackwings are responsible for their deaths?"

"The Blackwings did kill Gnaw and Octavius, probably Crysta, too. As for the other three, that falls under club business, which I'm not discussing with you. I will say I don't agree with his reasoning, and I've told him as much every time he brings it up."

The door to the storage shed flew open revealing a wide-eyed Batta. "Prez, you need to step outside and take this call," he said and thrust a phone toward me. "I'll stay with Aim."

I snatched the phone from his hand and stepped outside. "Copper Black."

"Prez, we found Layla in the Disciples' clubhouse. She's in the cage with Coal, and we're on our way back," Tiny blurted.

I expected as much, but it still wasn't easy to hear. "Is she okay? Did they hurt her? Where was she?"

"From what I could tell, she was a little banged up, but okay. She was alert and talking when I carried her out. I didn't take the time to really look her over or ask her any questions. As soon as I got her hands free, we hauled ass out of there."

"The fuck you mean about her hands?" I growled.

"Prez, we found her locked in Aim's bedroom.

Her wrists were chained to the headboard," he said, his voice full of anger and concern.

I didn't want to ask, but I had to know before I went back to face Aim. "Was she clothed?"

I heard Tiny swallow thickly. "She had on a bra and panties. Nothing else. Coal gave her his shirt to wear.

"Motherfucker!" I bellowed. I heaved in a few lungfuls of air in a vain attempt to get myself under control. "I gotta go, Tiny. I need to talk to her."

"Quick side note, Coal found out who she is. He didn't say as much, but the boy is pissed."

"He can be pissed all he wants, but his shit will have to take a number and get in line. Get her back here safe, brother. See you soon."

I ended the call and immediately dialed Coal. "Copper?" Layla's sweet voice filled my ear.

"Locks, baby, are you okay?"

She sniffled and cleared her throat. "Yeah, I am now. They said they were taking me to you. Please don't send me somewhere else." The desperation in her plea broke my heart.

"I won't, Locks. They're bringing you to me. Layla, baby, did they hurt you?"

"No, not like that. Just a few bumps and bruises," she murmured.

Relief like I have never felt before washed over me. I wanted to speak, to say something comforting to her, but my throat was clogged with emotion. Only a strangled sound came out when I opened my mouth.

Layla gasped, "Copper, I'm okay. I promise. Once again, you saved me. My knight in guns and leather."

"I don't know what I would've done if—" I whispered.

She cut me off, "Don't. We're not going there. I can't handle it, and neither can you."

"Okay, baby." I was about to end the call when I realized I had something to ask her. "Hey, Locks, do you know who took you?"

She sighed, "Not exactly. I know it was one of the Disciples of Death. I don't know which one took me, but there was one guy who came into the room a few times, and he's the one who blacked my eye."

The growl I emitted was nothing short of feral. "Who. The. Fuck. Put. Their. Hands. On. You?"

"His cut said he was Asp, the VP."

"Okay, okay," I said and blew out a breath as I tried to rein in my temper. "You and Coal stay safe, and I will see you soon."

"Oh, one more thing. I overheard something I think you should know about."

"I'm listening."

"When I was starting to wake up, that Asp guy was in the room talking to someone on the phone. I was still kind of out of it, but he said something about making them pay the way Gnaw made his brother and sister pay. Why would he be talking about my, um, you know, the man who impregnated my mother?"

"I don't know, Locks. Let's talk about it in person. You know, unsecured phone lines and all," I lied. I needed to get off the phone with her and figure out what in the ever-loving fuck was going on.

"Okay, I'll see you soon," she said and ended the call.

I spun on my heel and stomped back to the storage shed heading straight to Aim. Getting right in his face, I asked, "Can you prove you weren't at your clubhouse last night?"

He met my stare with fear-filled eyes, "Yes, I

can. My daughter is sick. I've been at the hospital with her for the last two days."

I got the name of the hospital and called Spazz to have him tap into their surveillance cameras. Unfortunately, he was on his bike riding back from the Disciples' clubhouse, and this couldn't wait for him to get back. Well, it could, but I didn't want to wait. Instead, I called Phoenix's tech guy, Byte, and asked him to do it. It took him less than ten minutes to confirm Aim had been at the hospital for the last two days until he left for the meeting.

Back in the storage shed, I studied Aim. He seemed frustrated, not scared or angry as one would expect. I couldn't put my finger on it, but something wasn't adding up. And why would he put up with so much disrespect and disobedience from his Vice President? Aim had every right to strip Asp of his title and his patch for his recent activities.

Aim sighed in exasperation. "Sounds like you found your girl at my clubhouse. Is she okay?"

"Claims it's just bumps and bruises. I won't know for sure until I see her myself."

"Asp is fucked in the head, but I can assure

you, he wouldn't force himself on her. That's the one line he won't cross."

I scoffed, "Yeah, your word doesn't mean shit to me."

"Fair enough."

For the next half hour, I silently stood in the storage shed with Aim, leaning against the wall and waiting. I hoped he would grow uncomfortable with the silence and my unwavering scrutiny and start volunteering information. Either he didn't have anything to share, or he was using the same tactic I was because he didn't utter a word.

The shed door eased open, and Tiny stuck his head around the corner. "Prez, can yo—oomph."

Tiny stumbled to the side as a blur of blonde hair and bare legs barreled past him. I barely had time to brace before Layla launched herself into my arms. "Copper!" she cried and buried her face in my neck.

"Layla," I breathed. With one arm under her ass and one around her shoulders, I held her to me as tightly as I could without hurting her. Aim sucking in a sharp breath faintly registered, but I was too consumed with Layla to acknowledge his presence in the room.

I loosened my hold on her and pulled back. "Baby, let me see your face."

Slowly, she raised her head and met my eyes. One look at her swollen and bruised face spawned a rage so intense I had to put her down and push her away from me so I didn't hurt her. I didn't lose my temper often, but when I did, everything in my path was at risk.

Tiny moved to push Layla behind him as Batta appeared and blocked the doorway. I was about to go at it with Batta and physically move him out of my way when Layla's words had me freezing mid-stride.

"You!" she shrieked. "What the fuck are you doing here?"

I turned to see her pointing a shaking finger and glaring at Aim. "You know him?"

"He, h-he," she swallowed and straightened her spine. "The night I escaped from Hastings and Hensley, he was the guard." She turned her tear-filled eyes to me. "I thought they were all arrested. Why is he here?"

I took a step closer to her, and it killed me when she flinched and took two steps away from me. "No! Don't come any closer."

"Tiny, get her out of here, right the fuck now,"

Batta yelled with his big hands pushing against my chest.

"Don't you fucking touch her," I roared and shoved Batta.

Suddenly, my back was against the wall, and Judge's forearm was pressing hard against my throat. "She doesn't need to be in here, Prez, and you know it. I ain't stopping you from whooping his ass. I'm just not going to let you do it in front of her."

Aim cleared his throat. When he spoke, his tone was much more authoritative, "Grab a chair and have a seat. I can explain everything."

27

COPPER

othing could have shocked me more than the words that came from Aim's mouth. While I wanted to believe he was lying, I knew he wasn't. What he said connected all the dots, and he claimed to have the documentation to verify he was telling the truth.

"I don't know how you want to play this, but it would be best if what was said in this room stays in this room for the time being," Aim said.

"I can't let you and Asp walk out of here without giving my brothers an explanation. And quite frankly, I'm not comfortable keeping it from them, especially my officers."

"I get that, but the more people who know, the greater chance this has of blowing up in all of our faces. I can't let that happen when I'm this close to the end."

"About that. What happens when all is said and done?"

Aim shrugged. "I don't know. It won't be my decision to make. It's not important right now anyway. We have more pressing issues to work on."

I nodded and rubbed my chin with my thumb and forefinger. "Here's what I'm thinking. You let me tell my officers what's going on. Then, we agree to let you and Asp go and tell you where the guns are stashed in exchange for a truce and money to repair the damage done to my clubhouse. Oh, and you let us beat on your VP for taking my Old Lady before he receives whatever punishment you're going to dole out."

He looked at me skeptically. "You think your brothers will go for that? Seems like a slap on the wrist given the circumstances."

"That's why I want my officers to know the truth. They're the ones who vote on club decisions. The club members have to go along with whatever we decide. They may not like it, but they trust me and my officers to lead them."

"Okay, I'll agree to letting your officers know."

He paused and squirmed in his chair. "There's something else you should know, but only you. If that's not something you can handle, I'll keep it to myself for now."

I didn't know if I could handle anything else. He'd already dropped a massive bomb on me, and he wanted to add to it. I pinched the bridge of my nose when I felt the twinge of an oncoming headache. "Is whatever you have to say going to affect the safety of my club and its members?" He shook his head. "All right, go ahead."

"My father died in a freak accident at work when I was seven years old. My mother passed away a few years ago. I was the only family she had, so she left everything to me including a safe deposit box. I went to see what she kept in it and found some documents indicating my biological father was not the man that raised me. So, I started digging for more information, and that's what ultimately led to me being involved in this whole situation," he explained as if he had repeatedly rehearsed the conversation.

"What part of that was necessary for me to know?" I asked.

"This part. My biological father's name was Jimmy Burnett."

I was on my feet and pacing before he finished the last name. "No. You can't be serious."

"I wish I wasn't. Well, I used to wish that until I found out about Annabelle and Layla," he said solemnly.

"How long have you known about them?"

"I found out about Annabelle not long after I found out Jimmy was my father. I wanted to approach her first before I confronted Jimmy, but I couldn't find her. It was like she vanished into thin air. I continued to dig for information about her, and I grew more and more certain something wasn't right. That's when I turned my attention to Jimmy. I got in with the club and kept my true identity to myself. Sorry, I'm getting off track. I found out about Layla when Jimmy kidnapped and sold her. At that point, I was in too deep to do anything about it, so I made sure to protect her as best I could. Then, she disappeared. Seems both of my sisters have a knack for vanishing without a trace."

"And you want me to keep your true identity from my Old Lady? From my club? From the President of the entire club?" I shook my head as I continued to pace. "I'm not sure I can do that, man."

"If it gets out that Annabelle and Layla are my half sisters and Gnaw's daughters, Asp will set his sights on them. His fucked-up mind will consider them Disciples by blood. He'll want them with the Disciples. Fuck man, he's already kidnapped Layla."

"Fuckin' A. I don't know how much more of this shit I can take," I mumbled. "Wait. He doesn't know about them?"

"No, he doesn't. From what I gathered, no one in the club knew about any of Gnaw's children, and they still don't."

Damn it. Keeping something from the club went against every one of my principles, but I couldn't see another way around it. I had to keep Aim's relation to Annabelle and Layla to myself for the time being. "I'm not in the habit of keeping secrets and lying to my club and my family, but I understand the necessity. How about you and I pretend the last five minutes of this conversation never happened?"

Aim nodded. "Sounds good."

"I need to secure Asp and get my officers in here so we can vote," I said and left the storage shed.

After assigning Coal to stay with Layla and

the remainder of the Croftridge brothers to guard Asp, my officers followed me into the storage shed.

"New information has been brought to my attention. We need to discuss it and make some decisions. This information is sensitive and cannot be discussed outside of this room."

"No disrespect, Prez, but why are we discussing sensitive matters in front of him?" Batta asked, nodding toward Aim.

"I'll explain that. Let me get through it all before you start asking questions." I took a moment to meet each set of eyes before I continued.

"Aim is not a federal agent, but he is working undercover to take down the Disciples. His focus has been on their involvement in illegal gun trading. Previously, their club dealt with Octavius. Since his disappearance and death, they had to find a new supplier, and they managed to get in deep with a large organized crime ring. Aim and his team are close to taking them down. Having said that, it's also come to light that Asp was behind the attack on the clubhouse, the envelopes we received, and Layla's kidnapping. He acted without Aim's knowledge or approval. So, we have some decisions to make. As I explained to Aim, I can't let them walk out of here without raising suspicions from all parties involved. However, I'd prefer to let the agents and officers do the dirty work and keep our hands clean. My suggestion is to establish a 'truce' with the Disciples. We'll give them the location of the guns, and they'll foot the bill for the repairs to our clubhouse. Oh, and we get to play with Asp for kidnapping my Old Lady. Then, he'll be punished by the Disciples for disobeying his President and almost causing them a world of trouble since his actions are the sole reason we took their shipment."

I expected the room to erupt in angry shouts and outbursts. I was prepared for chaos. I was not prepared to be met with wide, blinking eyes and complete silence. "Does your silence mean you guys are ready to vote?"

That's when they exploded. The shouts of outrage, muttered curses, and statements of disbelief blended into indecipherable noise. Despite the throbbing in my head, I gave them time to unleash their thoughts and emotions.

When several minutes passed and they still

hadn't calmed, I whistled loudly and shouted, "Enough!" The room fell silent.

"I get it, brothers, and I'm right there with you, but we don't have time to argue this in circles. We're either on board or we're not. Time to vote. Yay if you agree with the plan; nay if you don't," I barked.

I wasn't surprised when every officer voted in favor of the plan. Even when it wasn't what they personally wanted, my officers would always go with what was best for the club. "Thanks, brothers. Now, let's go have some fun with Asp."

28

LAYLA

I was sitting at a table in a rundown bar with my nephew, who I'd just met, with only his t-shirt covering my bra and panties. And, a man who participated in abducting me—not once, but twice—was tied to a chair in a shed behind said rundown bar. Copper had a lot of explaining to do, and the longer he took, the more pissed off I became.

The silence between Coal and I was awkward and beginning to grate on my nerves. I cleared my throat to get his attention. "If I didn't say it earlier, thank you for finding me and bringing me back."

He nodded and replied curtly, "Yep, you're welcome."

"If I've done something to offend you—" I started, but he cut me off.

"Listen, lady, in the last year I've met my biological mother, father, twin sister, and half brother. Now an aunt shows up. Excuse the fuck out of me for being tired of unknown family members popping up left and right. Because, more times than not, they bring a fuckload of problems with them," he spat.

Before I could utter a word, Coal was pulled from the booth by a furious Copper. "Who the fuck you think you're talking to, boy? Family or not, I'm the President of this club, and she's my Old Lady. You show her the respect she deserves."

Coal's shoulders visibly slumped. "You're right. I'm sorry, Copper." He turned to face me. "I'm sorry, Layla. I had no right to snap at you."

"Go take Edge's place and send him over here," Copper ordered.

Coal left immediately. "What was that about?" I asked, shocked by the entire scene.

Copper sighed. "It's not my story to tell, but the short version is Coal's immediate family was separated years ago and recently found each other. All of them went through some difficult situations related to their separation, including

Coal almost dying when he took three bullets to the gut. It doesn't excuse his behavior, but his reaction to you, especially given how he found you, is not surprising."

"He thinks I'm going to put his family in danger."

"Can't say for sure without asking him, but that'd be my best guess."

I slumped back in my seat. Even though I hadn't met Annabelle yet, I didn't want to put her or her family in danger, and that's exactly what I had unknowingly done. Hell, it was her own son who rescued me after a rival motorcycle club kidnapped me in the middle of the night.

"Stop that shit right now." Copper's harsh command had my head shooting up. "I know what you're thinking, and the answer is no. You're not going anywhere. None of this is your fault."

I could only blink. How could he possibly know what I was thinking?

He moved to stand. "I've got a few things to wrap up, and then I'll take you back to the clubhouse." He turned and motioned for someone to come over. "This is Edge. You okay sitting with him while I finish up?"

"Yes, I'm sure I'll be fine," I said softly.

He leaned in to give me a quick kiss on the lips, and then he was gone.

A friendly looking young man took his seat. "Hi, Layla. I'm Edge from the Croftridge chapter of Blackwings."

For the next hour, I sat with Edge while he did a phenomenal job of making small talk and keeping me distracted.

Finally, Copper came back to the table. "You ready to go, Locks?" he asked as he extended his hand to me.

I felt my cheeks heat. "Uh, I'm not exactly dressed to ride on your bike."

He smirked, "Know that. We're taking the cage, and Coal's going to bring my bike back to the clubhouse. We'll stop by my house on the way so you can get some clothes."

After a shower at Copper's house, I put on a fresh set of clothes and looked around to see if there was anything else I should take with me. My eyes landed on Luke's business card on the dresser. I grabbed it and shoved it into my pocket before letting Copper know I was ready to go to the clubhouse.

When we entered the common room, all of the guys were on their feet and bombarding me with questions about my well-being. After assuring them I was okay, I excused myself to Copper's room as I was in desperate need of a nap.

I had just crawled under the covers and gotten comfortable when I heard the door creak open. "You okay, baby?" Copper asked.

"Yeah, I'm just really tired. I think they may have drugged me at some point."

"I'm going to have Splint come in and check you over."

I didn't bother arguing with him. I didn't have the energy for such a futile endeavor.

Splint came in a few minutes later looking concerned. "We should stop meeting like this," I joked, trying to lighten the moment.

He grinned. "You got that right."

He examined my bruised and swollen face, checked my vital signs, and had me follow a series of commands I thought were ridiculous. Finally, he told Copper he thought I would be fine, but I needed to be checked on every hour and woken up every two hours while I slept.

Copper took a seat at the edge of the bed. "Do you need me to get you anything? Something to eat or drink?"

"Why did you have that man tied to a chair

in a shed behind a bar?" I finally asked the question that had been eating away at my insides since I was physically removed from the shed.

His face flashed with regret, maybe, before he masked it. "Club business, Locks."

I bit my tongue and asked my next question, even though I already knew the answer. "Why did that other club take me?"

He visibly grimaced. "Club business."

I was out of bed and on my feet in a flash. "So, let me see if I have this correct. I was taken from a place I thought was safe by a club that has a problem with you and your club. Then, I'm rescued and brought back to you only to find you in a room with a man tied to a chair who previously played a part in holding me captive and you don't think any of that is MY BUSINESS?!?"

"Locks, calm down."

"No. Fuck that and fuck you. This is bullshit, and you know it."

"I'm sorry, Locks. I really am," he said, and a part of me really wanted to believe him.

"Just leave," I said as I crawled back into the bed and turned away from him.

"Baby, I want to tell you, but I can't, not right now."

"Then leave me alone until you can." I kept my back to him and held myself very still until I heard the door open and close. Then, the tears came.

SHOUTING FROM SOMEWHERE IN THE CLUBHOUSE woke me.

"Where is she?" a woman demanded.

"Mom, you know you can't come in here making demands—"

"Jonah Jackson, if you don't shut your mouth this instant, I'll slap the taste right out of it. I am your mother, first and foremost. Just tell me where Layla is, and I'll be out of your hair."

I slipped out of the room and peeked around the corner to see a very pissed off Leigh standing in the middle of the common room. I cleared my throat and said, "I'm right here."

Her head whipped around, and she gasped when her eyes landed on me. She came at me with her arms extended. "Oh, sweetheart, are you okay?"

I went to her and gladly accepted her comfort. "Yeah. I'm sore and a bit sleepy, but I think I'm otherwise okay."

"Thank goodness. I've been so worried about you. When I couldn't find you—" her words broke off as she choked on a sob. She took a deep breath and continued, "I knew something terrible had happened." Shaking her head, she managed to rein in her emotions. "Come on, honey, let's get you back in bed, and I'll make you something to eat."

Not wanting to be in the presence of the men any longer than I had to, I was quick to take her up on her offer.

Once we were back in Copper's room, I asked, "What are you doing here?"

"When I realized you were missing, I called Jonah immediately. He told me they knew where you were and were en route to get you. However, he failed to let me know anything after that and didn't answer his phone when I called fifteen times. So, I picked up my keys and let the girls know I was heading to the clubhouse to find out what was going on for myself. Andrea, in no uncertain terms, told her husband he would accompany me or his dick would only see the inside of his palm for the foreseeable future. He readily agreed, and here we are."

I smiled. "I'm sorry you were worried, but I'm so glad you came." I felt tears prick the backs of my eyes as I struggled with my emotions.

Leigh took a seat beside me on the bed. "Did something happen to you that I don't know about?" Leigh asked carefully.

I quickly shook my head. "No, nothing like that. It's just, well, Copper is keeping things from me, and I'm not handling it well."

"What do you mean? What is he keeping from you?"

"He won't tell me why another club kidnapped me. Also, when Coal found me and brought me back, Copper had a man tied to a chair in a shed behind some dive bar. That man was one of the guards holding me prisoner when my father sold me to human traffickers. When I asked why he was there, Copper told me it was club business."

Leigh grimaced. "I used to hate when my husband would utter those dreaded words to me. I'll tell you what he told me when I raised hell about it. It didn't make it okay with me, but it did help me understand better. So, basically, he said he couldn't tell me club business for my own safety. For example, let's say one or more of the guys committed a crime they were later arrested for. If I knew nothing about it, I couldn't be held accountable for it. Plausible deniability or something like that. On the flip side, it is somewhat of a common rule amongst MC's to keep their women in the dark. It keeps other MC's from targeting the women and trying to get information from them."

"That makes sense, but the difference here is, I was the one kidnapped by the other MC, and I saw the man in the chair. I have no grounds to deny anything, and my safety was already put in jeopardy."

"I don't disagree with you. How did you and Copper leave things?"

"He said he wanted to tell me and he eventually would, but he couldn't right now. I told him to get out and leave me alone until he could tell me."

She patted my leg and rose to her feet. "Well, sounds to me like you could use some comfort food." With that, she left the room, leaving her purse on the bed.

I felt a slight tinge of guilt for digging through

her personal belongings, but it was my only option. I quickly found her cell phone and did a silent happy dance when I discovered it wasn't locked with a password. Reaching into my back pocket, I pulled out the card with Luke's contact information and dialed.

"Luke Johnson," he answered on the second ring.

"Luke, this is Layla, Layla East. I have some information for you."

29

COPPER

"She okay?" I asked Leigh when she came out of my room.

"She's rightfully upset. I'm going to make her something to eat and see if I can get her to take a nap," she said.

"She tell you about what happened?" I asked, desperate to know where her head was.

Leigh shook her head sadly. "Copper, I love you like you were my own son, but I won't be getting in the middle of your relationship with Layla. What she says to me, stays with me. Same goes for you. If you want answers, go talk to her."

I nodded and stepped aside so she could continue on to the kitchen. I knew Layla was pissed, and I couldn't say I blamed her. I wanted to tell her everything, but I couldn't. Not yet. I couldn't risk Aim's secret getting out, thereby putting her and Annabelle, not to mention Aim, in danger. I could only hope she would understand and forgive me once the truth was out.

Needing a distraction, I went to my office to get some work done. Unfortunately, I couldn't focus on anything as my mind kept straying to thoughts of Layla. I picked up the phone to call Phoenix, hoping he could give me some advice on how to handle the situation, but I quickly canceled the call when I realized I couldn't talk to him about it either.

Frustrated didn't even begin to cover how I was feeling, and sitting in my office was doing nothing to help. So, I got my ass up and went to help with repairing the clubhouse. Hopefully, the physical activity would keep my mind busy until I was too exhausted to do anything other than sleep.

POUNDING ON MY OFFICE DOOR WOKE ME THE

next morning. "Open up, Prez! It's urgent!" Judge shouted through the door.

I jumped up and yanked the door open. For Judge to say something was urgent, it was more than fucking urgent. The big bastard barely gave me time to get out of the way before he charged into the room and went straight to the television hanging on the wall in my office. He flipped to a news channel and turned up the volume.

—arrested this morning. He has been linked to the human trafficking operation ran by former Senator Lawrence Hastings and businessman Harold Hensley. Sources tell us he is also the President of a local outlaw motorcycle gang—

"Fuck!" I roared. "How the fuck did that happen?" My own question was answered moments later when the news showed a video clip of a handcuffed Aim walking in front of federal agents, one of which I recognized immediately.

Luke Johnson.

Without another word, I blew past Judge and ran down the hall. Throwing open the door to my room, I found exactly what I expected. No sign of Layla.

My fist hit the wall, over and over, until I was

physically restrained. Even then, I fought to rein in my emotions.

It was the sound of a female sobbing that brought me back to the present. I struggled against the hold Tiny and Batta had on me. I needed to know who was crying. Was it Layla?

My eyes frantically darted around the room, scanning and dismissing familiar faces, until my gaze landed on Leigh. She was tucked under Judge's arm with one hand cupped over her mouth while tears streamed down her face.

I locked eyes with her. "Where is she?" I pleaded, not caring one bit how desperate I sounded.

She shook her head. "I don't know, Copper. I didn't know she was gone until just now."

I twisted and jerked my shoulders. "Let me go," I demanded.

The two fuckers holding me back looked to Judge for approval, and I almost lost it again. "I am your President. Let me fucking go, NOW!"

Tiny and Batta released me, and Judge stepped in front of his mother. "Are you serious right now? Do you actually think I would hurt her?"

Judge didn't hesitate to respond. "No, I don't

think you'd intentionally hurt her, but you weren't exactly in your right mind just now."

"When was the last time you saw her, Leigh?"

"Last night around nine o'clock. She said she was ready to go to bed, so I left her and went to Judge's room," Leigh said.

"All right. Judge, check the camera feed. We need to know if she left on her own or if she was taken." I pinched the bridge of my nose and shook my head. This couldn't be happening.

"Hey, Prez, did you see this?" Batta asked, pointing at something on the nightstand.

I walked over to find a business card with Luke's contact information on it. "Well," I sighed, "I guess we know who told him about Aim."

Without hesitation, I pulled my phone out of my pocket and dialed the number on the card.

"Johnson," he answered gruffly.

"Where the fuck is she?" I demanded.

He cleared his throat. "I'm sorry. You'll have to be a little more specific."

"Cut the shit, Luke. Tell me where Layla is."

"Ah, Copper. I've been expecting your call. I'm not telling you where she is, though."

"And why the fuck not?" I growled.

"Because I'm not at liberty to share any details

related to an active case," he replied automatically.

My grip tightened around my phone, causing the plastic to creak. "Luke," I warned.

"Look, man, she's safe, and that's all I can tell you. I've gotta go," he said and disconnected the call.

Judge returned to the room. "Looks like she voluntarily left around midnight. She walked to the gate carrying a bag and got into a black SUV."

I held my phone up and shook it. "Yeah, I just got off the phone with Luke. He knows where she is. The fucker won't tell me shit, but he says she's safe."

"Whatcha want us to do, Prez?"

I shook my head. "There's nothing we can do, not about her anyway. Let's get back to work on finishing the repairs. We'll also need to stay extra-vigilant now that Asp doesn't have anyone to answer to."

I left the room and walked back to my office. I needed a few minutes alone to process what had just happened and to get my anger under control. Closing the door behind me, I turned and stopped dead in my tracks.

"Have a seat, little cousin. I think you and I need to have a chat," Phoenix said from the chair behind my desk.

Fuck me. He was obviously pissed, but I didn't know if it was about Coal, Layla, Aim, or something else. I took a seat and carefully studied his face. Unfortunately, his expression was giving nothing away, other than irritation. I crossed my arms over my chest and asked, "What's this about?"

Phoenix straightened in my chair and glared at me. "You really want to play dumb? Fine. I don't have time for this bullshit back and forth, so I'll lay it out for you. It's about you keeping shit from your President, your brothers, and your family. I know about Layla's kidnapping, and I know she called Luke for help. Hell, I even know where she is right now." I opened my mouth to interrupt, but he held up his hand, and the look on his face told me it would be in my best interest to let him finish. "I know all about Aim—his real name, his fake name, his undercover work, everything. And, I know about Coal asking you to patch over. What I don't know is why you kept all that from me?"

I looked to my feet and took in a deep breath

before I started explaining. "Let's start with Coal. I didn't tell you because that's not how we do things, which is exactly what I told him. I said I understood why he came to me first, but I told him he had to talk to you, get your approval, and then ask me. He said he would speak to you as soon as he got back to Croftridge. I don't really see how you have a problem with that."

"Never said I had a problem with it. Keep going," he said gesturing with his hands.

"I didn't tell you about Layla, because I haven't had a chance to. Honestly, I just found out she called Luke and asked for his help before I walked in here. I didn't intentionally keep the kidnapping from you, but it was one thing after another from the moment we found out she was taken. Now, Aim, yeah, I did intentionally keep that from you. I didn't want to, but he argued a good point. I did it for Annabelle's and Layla's safety. He said they would be in serious danger if Asp found out they were his sisters. He said—"

I was cut off when Phoenix got to his feet with a roar and cleared the top of my desk with a sweep of his hands. "The fuck did you just say?"

"Uh, he's their half brother, younger than Annabelle, older than Layla," I said carefully. I thought he said he knew everything. "You didn't know?"

"No, I didn't fucking know! I was talking about his involvement in the undercover operation. How do you know that's true?"

"I don't know for sure. It's not like he had the documents on him to prove it, though he did claim to have that documentation, but I didn't think he was lying. He was livid when he found out Asp had taken Layla, and he was genuinely concerned about her well-being, Annabelle's, too," I explained. "No one besides me knows he's their brother, and only my officers know he is working undercover."

"That's not entirely true anymore. I know, as well as my officers. And Luke will know in the very near future if he doesn't already."

"What? How did you even find out?"

Phoenix smirked. "Did you bother to ask who he was working with?"

I shook my head. "No, I didn't ask. He mentioned it wasn't the FBI and it wasn't local law enforcement—"

"He's working with a team that hired Wave as an independent consultant. He called me when he heard about the arrest." Fuck. I should've known

Wave was somehow involved. He used to run an independent special operations team, for lack of a better description, that was contracted out for particularly difficult cases. He retired years ago, but still did some independent consulting on cases from time to time. Coincidentally, Luke used to be on his team.

"Did Luke know Aim was working with the good guys?" I asked.

"No, he didn't, and he's beyond pissed about it."

I dropped my head and blew out a slow breath. "So, what do we do now?"

"Huh, I thought you'd be demanding to know where Layla is," Phoenix mumbled.

I raised my head and met his eyes. "You wouldn't be sitting here right now if you knew she wasn't safe. Do I want to know where she is? Yes. Do I think you'll tell me? No. All that matters right now is that she's out of harm's way."

Phoenix studied me for a few moments before he nodded and answered my previous question. "There's not a whole lot you can do. Aim can't be released without his cover being blown. You can't go after the club because the feds will be watching their every move. At this point, your hands are tied."

Well, wasn't that just fan-fucking-tastic? I had to sit idly by while a psycho, who was now in charge of an outlaw motorcycle club, ran around free, planning to do who knows what. All while my girl was hidden away in an unknown location, probably thinking the worst of me.

Not knowing where her head was at was killing me. Did she think I didn't care about what happened to her? Did she think I was okay with human trafficking? Did she know that I was in love with her?

There was no way I could sit around twiddling my thumbs waiting for something to happen, for someone else to take care of the problem. No, I needed to come up with a plan so I could get my woman back.

30

LAYLA

A knock at the door had me jumping three feet in the air and screaming bloody murder. Supposedly, only two people knew my whereabouts, and they both had keys. No one should be knocking. And since I screamed like a banshee, I couldn't pretend no one was home. That didn't mean I had to open the door, though.

I tiptoed through the living room and peeked through the blinds to see who was knocking on the door. A man I had never seen before was standing on the front porch. A huge man. And he was looking right at me. I jolted away from the window, tripped on the rug, and fell on my ass.

He knocked again. "Open up, Layla! I know you're in there."

Fuck. Fuck. Fuckity fuck. How did he know my name?

"No fucking way, man. I'm going to give you five seconds to get off my porch before I start shooting through the door," I yelled. Did I have a gun? No, but he didn't know that.

He responded with a chuckle, which unnerved me even more. I ran back to the kitchen and grabbed the biggest knife I could find while frantically trying to think of a place to hide. This was a safe house, for fuck's sake. How did it not have a panic room?

I darted around the corner and headed for the stairs when arms wrapped around my chest from behind and halted my forward momentum. "I'm not going to hurt you."

"Says the man who just broke into my house!" I screamed and moved my arm forward, preparing to plunge the knife into his side. Before I could swing my arm back, I flew across the room and hit the wall with a thud, the knife clattering to the floor.

"Fuck! Shit! Are you okay? I didn't mean to push you that hard, but fuck if I was going to let you stab me," the man said from the other side of the room. What the hell was going on?

He held his hands up in front of him, but didn't try to approach me. "I'm Phoenix. Phoenix Black. Did Copper tell you about me?"

I straightened myself and glared at him. "Yes, he did. I can see being an asshole runs in the family."

He had the decency to look embarrassed. "I'm truly sorry. I know you're a runner, and I didn't want you to take off before I had a chance to talk to you."

"I've ran because I had to, not because it's a compulsive habit," I spat.

"Fair enough. Are you sure you're okay?"

"I'm fine. What is it you need to talk to me about?"

"Can we sit?"

"Hell, no. You stay right where you are and start talking."

He sighed and rubbed his chin with his thumb and forefinger, just like I'd seen Copper do numerous times. "The man Copper had tied up in the shed, the guard who let you get away from the stables, was working undercover to bring down an outlaw motorcycle club, the same one that took you. He's also your half brother."

"WHAT?!" I shrieked and placed my hand over my chest. He was lying. He had to be. There was no way my own brother would have held me hostage while waiting for me to be sold. Who was I kidding? Of course, he would. My own fucking father sold me. It would stand to reason his son would help.

"He's the reason nothing happened to you while you were there. He's also the reason you were able to escape. Did you really think your little trick with the hay would keep a grown man from chasing after you?"

Actually, I did, until he said that. "I-I…" I had no words. My mind was a whirlwind of activity, yet my mouth refused to work.

"He told Copper who he was that day in the shed, and he made Copper promise not to tell anyone. He didn't want the men in his club finding out about you and Annabelle and coming after either one of you. Copper didn't want to do it, but he agreed to go against his morals and his club to protect you and your sister."

What had I done? I should have trusted Copper.

He said he would tell me what was going on when he could, but I didn't believe him. Too many men who supposedly cared about me had betrayed me, and I was determined not to let it happen again. But instead, I was the one who betrayed him. I covered my mouth with my hand and bent at the waist as a pain like no other hit my chest and a sob erupted from the very depths of my soul.

"Hey, you're not to blame. You didn't know, and you did what you had to do to keep yourself safe." I continued to cry and refused to look at him. "He's not mad at you. He's worried about you, but he understands."

That had me looking up. "He's not mad?" How could he not be mad?

Phoenix smiled and shook his head. "Not at you. He's pretty fucking pissed at Luke, for hiding you away, and at me, for not telling him where you were hidden, but he'll get over it."

I took a seat on one of the barstools and propped my head in my hands. "Why did you come? I mean, I know it was to tell me about Copper and my brother, but why?"

"I love my family. I couldn't have you thinking Copper was a bad man, and I certainly couldn't have you thinking Annabelle was married to the same kind of man. Plus, you're family, whether you like it or not, and I felt like you needed to be aware of how much danger is circling around you."

"Thanks, I think. I'm sorry, this is just a lot to take in. I just, what am I supposed to do now?" I asked, hating the desperation in my voice.

"Stay here, do what Luke tells you, and wait," he said simply.

"But what about Copper? And my brother? What's going to happen to him?"

"Your brother can't be released from custody without blowing his cover, but all charges will be dropped once the club has been dismantled. Copper will be fine. He's a big boy and can take care of himself. Now, I've got to get going. I have a very pregnant wife at home, and I don't like being this far away from her," he said with a proud smile.

"How is she? I can't wait to meet her," I blurted.

"She's good. Getting bigger every day, but I'll deny ever saying that if she gets wind of it. I can wait for you to meet her because she's going to kick my ass when she finds out I knew about you for weeks and didn't tell her."

"I'll tell her it was my fault. That I didn't want her to know about me until my life wasn't such a mess," I offered.

"I appreciate the offer, but it won't save my ass. I knew and didn't tell her; it doesn't matter the reason. Don't worry about it. After spending almost two decades apart, we don't stay upset with one another for long."

We said our goodbyes, and I made sure to check the locks on the doors and windows after he left. I wasn't sure how he got in, but I'd be damned if anyone else snuck in on me. Which was why Luke was beating on the door hours later. I may or may not have barricaded all entry points.

"What the hell, Layla?" Luke asked.

"Sorry about that. I didn't want anyone else surprising me."

His eyes widened. "Anyone else? Explain."

Well, shit. Phoenix didn't tell me to keep his visit a secret, but he didn't say it was okay to tell either. "Uh, I assumed you knew. Phoenix Black showed up a few hours ago."

Luke snorted. "Why doesn't that surprise me? Well, what did he have to say?"

Double shit. Was I supposed to tell him? I

assumed he was already aware of the information Phoenix shared. Maybe he wasn't. "Um…"

Luke sighed, "Let me guess. He told you about Aim's real identity and his involvement in the undercover operation?"

I exhaled in relief. "Yes, and he wanted to make sure I was aware of the potential danger."

Luke nodded. "You shouldn't be in any danger as long as you stay here and don't use any kind of electronics."

"Speaking of, how long will I have to stay here?"

He shrugged. "I don't know. Could be a few days, could be a few weeks."

A few weeks? I wanted to talk to Copper now, not a few weeks from now. What would things be like between us then? Phoenix said he wasn't mad at me, but I know I upset him by not trusting him. All because of my stupid father. If he wasn't already dead, I'd kill him myself.

31

COPPER

My head was pounding and my whole body ached, particularly my shoulders. I tried to roll to my side and couldn't. That had my head shooting up, despite the pain, and opening my eyes to total darkness. I tried to wriggle around, and that's when I realized I wasn't lying in bed but rather hanging from the ceiling, by chains.

Mother.

Fucker.

At least my feet were somewhat touching the floor.

No need to panic. I'd been in worse situations before and come out fine. I just needed to bide my time until I figured out how to get out of this mess or the cavalry showed up. And I knew they would. It was just a question of how long it would take for them to realize I was missing and find my location.

The sound of movement nearby caught my attention, and I automatically dropped my head and closed my eyes. I didn't want anyone to know I was awake yet. Unfortunately, that plan backfired, because I didn't see the fist to my gut coming. My head shot up again, and I heaved in a pained breath.

"Oh good, you're awake," a disgustingly familiar voice crowed.

I said nothing as I glared at Asp. I expected him to look haggard and stressed, but he looked calm and calculating, leaving me with an uneasy feeling.

He grinned, "I can see the wheels turning. Figured it out yet, Copper?"

No, motherfucker, I hadn't, but I wasn't about to tell him that.

He cackled like a maniac. "I've always loved story time. Do you? Most people do. So, let me tell you a little story. I think you'll enjoy it."

I don't know if he paused for dramatic effect or what, but it felt like it took him hours to start talking. I was looking forward to the distraction because the ache in my arms and shoulders was growing by the minute.

He laced his hands together and tapped his chin with his index fingers. "Hmm, where should I begin?"

I rolled my eyes. "At the fucking beginning, where most people do."

He threw his head back and laughed. I watched him closely. He was clearly insane, and that did not bode well for me.

"I never liked doing things the same as everyone else. So, I think I'll start at the end."

He paused and stared at me as if he was waiting for my agreement. Seriously? I was fucking hanging from the ceiling. It didn't matter if I agreed with him or not.

He huffed in annoyance at my lack of response, but finally started talking. "I've known about Aim's undercover work for quite some time, probably from the very beginning. It's the only reason I haven't killed that rat bastard. I'm not going down for murder. I'm not going down for shit. By the time they figure it out, I'll be long gone."

Well, I can't say I saw that coming. Looks like

we all underestimated Asp. It didn't matter. I just needed to stay alive and keep him talking until the club arrived.

"What will they figure out?" I asked.

"That Aim is an idiot, and they can't pin shit on me or anyone else in the club."

What? Of course, they could. Hell, my club even had proof of their gun running. Not to mention kidnapping Layla and bombing my clubhouse. I didn't ask, but I was sure Tiny and Coal could attest to their clubhouse being full of drugs. But it wasn't in my best interest to argue with him.

He cackled loudly before plowing his fist into my gut, again. "Whenever there's a problem with the club, who does everyone direct their attention to? The President. Not the VP. Not the officers. Just the President. So, I created some situations to keep the focus on Aim and not what I was really up to. I knew you fuckers didn't kill my brother and sister, but it was easy to point the finger at the Blackwings. Everyone was running around talking about how they didn't want a war with the big, bad Blackwings and worrying about how to keep the peace while I was busy selling off stolen guns and wiping out the club's funds."

Fuck. It was never a good sign when your captor started spilling all their secrets. It meant only one thing; he wasn't worried about me telling anyone else because he was planning on killing me before I had a chance.

"Now, let's have some fun. I have another surprise for you," he said with an evil glint in his eyes.

He nodded to a man standing guard by a door. Seconds later, the door opened, and my heart exploded in my chest. Layla and Annabelle were shoved into the room before the door slammed shut again.

"Surprise!" Asp shouted and threw his hands into the air.

Layla gasped and started toward me, but Asp put his hand out and roughly stopped her. "I don't think so, bitch. You stay right there and don't move."

Layla's eyes shot to mine, and I gave a slight nod, hoping she understood I wanted her to listen to him. Fuck. This was bad. He had to know Phoenix would be coming for Annabelle, and the feds would be after Layla the second they realized she was missing.

"Now, me and my insurance policies have

places to be. Story time's been fun, but we're at the end."

With that, he raised his gun and fired one shot directly into my chest. The last thing I heard were the screams of Layla and Annabelle.

32

LAYLA

"Noooo!" I screamed at the man who just shot the love of my life.

I tried to run to Copper, but the asshole with the gun yanked me back by my hair and threw me to the ground by Annabelle's feet.

Annabelle grabbed her stomach and bent forward moaning in pain. "Damn it," she cursed.

"Are you okay?" I asked.

"Gun in my boot. Two shots. Don't miss," she whispered. She continued clutching her stomach and groaned loudly. "Oh, I think the babies are coming!"

I moved closer to her and reached into her boot. When my hand wrapped around the cool metal, I didn't think about what I was doing, I just did it. I pulled the gun free, turned around, and shot Asp in the fucking face. Then, I turned and shot the bastard standing by the door.

"Get his gun," Annabelle yelled over her shoulder. She was beside Copper holding pressure to his chest.

I picked up Asp's gun and ran to her side. "I need you to figure out how to get him down while I hold pressure on his chest. Maybe Asp has the key in his pocket."

The last thing I wanted to do was dig through Asp's pockets, but I would do anything for Copper. Dropping to my knees beside what was left of Asp, I began searching for the key. Moments later, I had a set of keys in my hand as well as a cell phone.

I quickly placed a call to 9-1-1 and put it on speaker before I stood on a chair and started trying to unlock the cuffs around Copper's wrists.

"9-1-1, what is your emergency?"

"My boyfriend has been shot in the chest. I don't know where we are. We were kidnapped by a psycho. He needs help. Now!"

"Okay, ma'am. Is your boyfriend conscious?"

"No, he isn't. We're holding pressure and

trying to get him down. Please hurry," I screamed frantically.

"What's your name?" she asked.

"Focus on the cuffs. I'll talk," Annabelle said. "My name is Annabelle Black. My husband is Phoenix Black. His cousin, Copper Black, is the one who was shot. We were kidnapped by the Vice President of the Disciples of Death, Asp, who is now dead. Please call my husband. Also, call Luke Johnson with the FBI. He is working on this case. And please send another ambulance. I'm pregnant with twins, and my water just broke."

Just as Annabelle finished speaking, I unlocked the cuffs and fell to the floor with Copper. There was no way either of us could hold up his bulk, so I did my best to cushion his fall using my own body.

"I need you to hold pressure. I can't get down there to do it," Annabelle managed to say through panted breaths.

"Shit. Shitshitshitshitshit!" I screamed. "I don't know what to do!"

She held her stomach and wiped the sweat from her brow. "Hold pressure on his wound and make sure he's still breathing. Don't worry about me. I won't drop the babies before help gets here."

I turned back to Copper and tried to keep him from bleeding to death right before my very eyes. He was so still and so pale. "Please, Copper. Help is on the way. Just hang on a little bit longer. I'm sorry I left. I'm sorry I doubted you. I promise I won't ever do it again. Just, please be okay. Please," I pleaded through my tears. "I love you, Copper. I need you."

A commotion outside had me tensing. "Hand me that gun," Annabelle said between pants. I did as she asked and continued to hold pressure.

"Ma'am, the police are outside the building. Is it safe for them to enter?" the woman on the phone asked.

"We don't know. The two in the room with us are dead, but we don't know if any others were around," Annabelle answered.

"Okay, as soon as they have secured—" the woman was cut off when the door damn near flew off its hinges as Phoenix entered the room followed by a leather-clad army.

"Doll face! You okay, baby?" he asked Annabelle as he ran to her.

"Help Copper," she gritted out with her arms wrapped around her belly.

"Baby?" he asked.

"Her water broke," I supplied as I stood from my crouched position to give the paramedics room to work on Copper. "She's in labor."

"All right, let's go," he said and scooped Annabelle into his arms bridal style.

I startled when an extremely large hand landed on my shoulder. "Come on, Layla. Let's get you to the hospital," Batta said.

I nodded. "Okay, just one second."

I leaned over the stretcher the paramedics were strapping Copper to and placed a soft kiss on his pale lips. "I love you. Please be okay," I whispered and quickly stepped back.

Batta led me to an SUV and helped me into the passenger seat. As he started to pull onto the street, I finally took in my surroundings. "Where are we?"

Batta snorted. "The Disciples of Death's warehouse."

"How did you guys find us so fast?"

"Aim had the warehouse wired to help with the undercover investigation. Once he shared that information, we had our tech guys tap into the feed and saw Copper hanging from the ceiling. We didn't know he had you and Annabelle until Phoenix called and told us. By that time, we were already on our way."

"You knew he had Copper, but not me and Annabelle?" I asked, feeling a bit confused.

"You were supposedly at the safe house, so we had no idea you were missing. When Annabelle didn't return from her doctor's appointment, it didn't take Phoenix long to figure out something was wrong. He started making calls, and one of those calls was to Luke. When Luke couldn't get in touch with the guards at the safe house, they put two and two together."

I was suddenly pissed. "So, you guys waited for Phoenix to get here before you attempted to rescue your President?" If they hadn't waited, my man might not be knocking on death's door.

Batta pointed to the left, and I followed his finger. "See that helicopter over there? That belongs to Phoenix's Road Captain. They flew here. We saw them landing as we were coming down the road with the cops hot on our tails. We wouldn't have waited for Phoenix, and he wouldn't have wanted us to."

"I'm sorry. I shouldn't have assumed. I'm just

so damn worried about him," I said and then burst into tears.

Batta reached over and grabbed my hand, giving it a gentle squeeze. "We all are, sweetheart."

We rode the rest of the way in silence. I couldn't stop replaying Copper getting shot over and over in my mind. The way his body jerked when the bullet entered his chest. The spray of blood that hit the wall. The way his body slumped. The blood pooling on the concrete floor below his feet. The paleness of his skin. The coolness of his lips.

"We're here," Batta said, bringing me out of my continuous nightmare.

I stepped out of the SUV and immediately clutched my side as a sharp pain seared through my left torso. I bent forward and cried out in pain.

Batta was in front of me in a flash. "Layla, what's wrong?"

"My side," I gasped out. I tried to straighten, but it hurt too much. Hell, it hurt to even breathe.

I did let out a piercing scream when Batta unceremoniously scooped me into his arms and sprinted into the hospital. "Help me! She needs help!" he bellowed.

Splint materialized out of thin air. "What's going on?"

"Something with her left side, man," Batta said.

I felt hands tugging at my shirt, but I was more concerned with trying to breathe than anything else.

"Yo, I need a stretcher! We've got a woman with rib fractures and severe dyspnea, possible pneumothorax," Splint shouted.

Seconds later, Batta gently placed me on what I assumed was a stretcher, and they started to wheel me away. I met Batta's eyes and mouthed, "Copper," before he was out of sight. At his nod, I closed my eyes and succumbed to the pain.

33

LAYLA

A bubbling water sound woke me. When I opened my eyes and glanced around the room, it all came back to me in a rush. I knew I was in a hospital, but I wasn't sure why. Copper was the one who was hurt, not me.

I tried to sit up and moaned in pain. Batta appeared beside the bed and eased me back down. "You're okay, Layla, but you can't get up right now."

"Copper?" I croaked.

Batta picked up a hideously ugly pink cup and placed a straw at my lips. While I took a few sips of ice water, he told me, "He's still in surgery. They said it'll probably be two more hours before he's out."

"Is he going to be okay?"

Batta grimaced. "We don't know. They took him straight to the OR when he got here, and they wouldn't give any kind of prognosis when they called out and gave Phoenix an update."

"Annabelle?"

Batta smiled softly. "She's just fine and so are the babies. They were a little early and are in the NICU, but, from what Phoenix said, they were expecting that."

"Can I go see her?" I asked, hopefully.

Batta shook his head regretfully. "No, sweetie, you can't go anywhere until they remove your chest tube."

"My what?" I shrieked and immediately regretted it.

Splint, who I didn't even realize was in the room, answered, "Something punctured your left lung and caused it to collapse. They put in a chest tube to drain the air from around your lung so that it can re-inflate. You also have two fractured ribs on your left side, though neither of them caused your lung to collapse because they aren't displaced. From what the doctor said, you had a small puncture wound about two inches above your broken ribs. We're guessing you landed on a large nail when you and Copper fell."

I held up my hand to stop him from saying anything else as I fought to keep myself from vomiting all over him. I swallowed several times and took in a few slow breaths to get my nausea under control. Finally, I was able to say, "I don't need to know the details."

Before he could reply, a nurse walked into my room. "Hi, Mrs. Black. I'm Bridget, your nurse for the day. How are you feeling?"

My brows furrowed at the name, but I caught the slight shake of Splint's head and refrained from correcting her. "I'm in a lot of pain, and he's trying to make me puke," I said and pointed an accusatory finger at Splint.

His cheeks flushed and he stumbled over his words in his rush to explain. "I-I was just explaining her injuries to her and, um, what we thought happened to cause them."

Nurse Bridget nodded and turned her attention back to me. "I'll bring you something for pain and something for nausea. Is there anything else you need?"

"No, not unless you can tell me if Copper is out of surgery and doing okay."

"I'll see if I can get an update on your husband for you. I'll be right back."

"Husband?" I asked as soon as she left the room.

Batta shrugged. "I told them you were Copper's wife so we could get updates on him."

"Ah, thanks, I think."

When my nurse returned with my pain and nausea medicine, she also brought the news I desperately needed to hear. "Your husband is out of surgery and in recovery. They were able to remove the bullet and repair the damage. He'll be in recovery for a while, and then he'll be moved to the ICU."

"Thank you," I rasped as tears ran down my face.

She finished putting the medicines in my IV and gently patted my hand. "You're welcome, Mrs. Black. You try to get some rest, and I'll check on you in a bit. Press your call button if you need me." With that, she left the room, and I drifted off into a drug-induced sleep.

The next time I woke, Leigh and Judge were in my room. I shifted and cleared my throat. "How is he?"

Leigh was on her feet and beside my bed

before I finished my question. She brushed the hair from my face and gently cupped my cheek. "He's in the ICU, and they say he's stable. He hasn't woken up yet, but I think that's because of the medicine they're giving him."

"I want to see him. Please," I begged and tried not to cry. I needed to see him with my own eyes. I wanted to tell him that I loved him, and I would be waiting patiently for him to come back to me.

Leigh smiled. "You can't get out of bed yet, but before you go getting worked up, I have an idea. Jonah, hand me my phone." Leigh touched the screen a few times, and the sound of ringing filled the room shortly followed by Bronze's voice.

"Hey, Bronze, Layla wants to see Copper, but she's still on strict bed rest. I thought a video chat might pacify her, at least for a little while," she said and passed the phone to me.

"Hi, Bronze. How is he?"

"Hey, Layla, you doing okay?"

"I'd be much better if I could see him," I told him honestly.

He blew out a slow breath and nodded his head. "Yeah, okay. Listen, he lost a lot of blood, eally pale, and he has a lot of tubes and wires. I just want you to be prepared to see him like that, because I wasn't."

I couldn't stop the tears, but I squared my shoulders as best I could and nodded resolutely. "I'll be okay. Please, let me see him."

The screen changed, and my breath was stolen from me once again. Bronze was right; he was pale, far more so than I expected. He had a tube down his throat helping him breathe, as well as numerous other tubes and wires coming from underneath his blankets.

"Will you move me closer to his head?"

When only his face filled the screen, I began pouring my heart out, and I didn't care that everyone in my room, as well as his, could hear me. "Copper, baby, I need you to keep fighting. I'm okay, and Annabelle's okay. She had the babies, and Leigh says they're doing good, too. Your family and your club are here waiting for you to come back to us. I'm waiting for you to come back to me. I love you, Copper, and I need you by my side. I can't do this without you. I don't want to. I love you so much."

When Bronze started to move the phone, I asked, "Can I stay with him like this until I fall asleep again?"

"Of course, Layla. I'll leave the phone right where it is."

"Is that okay, Leigh?"

"Absolutely. Jonah, will you run down to the gift shop and see if they have a charger for my phone?"

"Sure thing, Mom. Be right back."

And that's how I spent the next three days of my hospital stay. When they finally removed my chest tube, I was on my feet and headed to the ICU before the doctor even left the room.

"Mrs. Black, I understand you're anxious to see your husband, but if you'll give us just a few minutes, I'll have one of the nurses bring a wheelchair to take you upstairs," the doctor offered.

I gestured over my shoulder with my thumb at Batta and Judge. "Can one of them carry me?"

The room erupted in laughter as my nurse pushed a wheelchair into my room. "There's no need for that. I knew you wouldn't wait long and have had this baby parked outside your room since my shift started this morning." She patted the seat, "Hop in, and I'll take you upstairs."

She wheeled me to a set of elevators that opened up inside the ICU. "These elevators are for patients only. Since you're technically still a patient, I thought it would be easier to take this route and bypass the waiting room filled with your friends and family members."

"Thank you. I do want to see them, but I want to see him first."

"That's what I thought. Real quick, you're still my patient, and I'm responsible for you. I have no problem with you staying up here with your husband as long as you promise to stay in this wheelchair and call me if you need anything."

"I promise," I told her, and I meant it. I wouldn't do anything to risk being taken away from Copper's side.

She left after she wheeled me into his room and parked me as close to his side as she could get me. I reached forward and took his hand in mine. "I'm here," I whispered.

And that's where I stayed until he woke up.

34

LAYLA

Five days had passed since Copper was shot, and he still hadn't woken up. The breathing tube had been removed, and everything looked good on paper; but, his eyes hadn't so much as twitched since I'd been by his side, and that worried me more than anything.

Did I hold enough pressure on his wound? Should I have tried to breathe for him before the paramedics arrived? Would chest compressions have helped him? Every moment I was awake, I replayed the events of that day over and over trying to figure out what I could have done differently.

With my head resting on his hand, I started to

drift off to sleep while I imagined his fingers sifting through my hair.

"Your thinking is making me tired."

My head shot up so fast I damn near knocked myself out of the chair. "Copper!" I shrieked and started pressing every button I could get my fingers on.

He closed his eyes, and I lost it. "No! Nononononono! Stay awake. Please, please, please," I wailed.

His eyes shot open again, but before I could breathe a sigh of relief, two nurses came running into his room.

"He's awake," I screeched and pointed at the wide-eyed man staring at the three of us.

"Bring it down a few notches," he said and squinted his eyes.

"How are you feeling, Mr. Black?" the nurse asked the first of many questions and proceeded to check everything she could possibly check on him.

I tried to be patient, but I was nearing my breaking point when the nurse finally left the room.

"I'm sorry," we both said at the same time.

"Come 'ere, Locks," he rumbled and patted the bed beside him.

With zero hesitation, I carefully crawled into the hospital bed with him and promptly turned into a sobbing mess. "I thought I lost you. He shot you, Copper. In the chest. There was so much blood, and we couldn't get you down, and—"

"I love you," he said, effectively shutting me up.

I raised my head so I could see his eyes. "I love you, too."

He grinned, "I know. I heard you that day in the warehouse. And I've heard you say it since then."

"What else have you heard?"

"A lot, but why don't you hit me with the highlights in case I missed something," he suggested.

"Okay, here goes. Asp shot you. I shot Asp. Annabelle went into labor. The babies are in the NICU. You fell on me and broke my ribs. A nail punctured my lung. Aim is still in police custody. And, I think that's it."

"How are your ribs?" he asked.

"Splint said they were cracked but not

completely broken, but they still hurt like a motherfucker if I move wrong," I told him honestly.

"Well, then, you should probably take it easy and get some rest," he said with a yawn, and before long, we were both asleep.

When I opened my eyes and saw Phoenix sitting in the chair that had been my home since I was allowed to leave my hospital room, I startled, which caused Copper to jolt. He let out a grunt of pain while I clutched my ribs and tried to take slow, easy breaths.

"Shit. I didn't mean to scare you. Can I do anything to help?" Phoenix asked.

"No," we both groaned.

Phoenix walked up to the side of the bed and grabbed Copper's hand. "Heard you were finally awake, but I had to see it for myself. You had us worried there for a minute."

"Yeah, I can admit getting shot in the chest scared the shit out of me, too," Copper said honestly. "How are Annabelle and the babies?"

Phoenix smiled. "They're all doing great. The twins are still in the NICU, but Annabelle's already been discharged from the hospital." He paused for a moment and rubbed his chin. "She's been asking about both of you. I was able to hold her off while she was still in the hospital, but now that she's been released, she'll be stopping by in between feeding times."

"What's the problem?" Copper asked.

"She doesn't know about Layla and Aim, yet, and I'm not—"

A throat cleared from behind Phoenix, startling the three of us. "Sorry to interrupt, but it sounds like my timing is perfect," Aim said with a grim look on his face.

"How so?" Copper asked.

Aim stepped into the room and ran his hand through his hair. "My little girl is sick. Has been for a while, and she needs a bone marrow transplant. We're on the registry, but we haven't found a match yet, and family members have a better chance of being a match, and—"

"You need us to get tested?" I asked.

"Please," he said with a desperation so great I felt tears sting the backs of my eyes.

Phoenix clapped Aim on the shoulder. "We'll tell her when she comes down. I know she won't have a problem with being tested, but I don't know if they'll let her since she just had the babies."

"Let me do what?" Annabelle asked.

"Doll face," Phoenix said and ushered her to a chair. "Everything okay upstairs?"

"Yes. Let me do what?" she asked again.

Phoenix blew out a breath and opened his mouth to speak, but I couldn't let him bear the brunt of the bombshell she was about to receive by being the one to tell her.

With no preamble, I sat up and extended my hand to her. "I don't believe we were formally introduced. I'm Layla East, your half sister."

She blinked, looked at my hand, turned to Phoenix, then back to my hand, and finally said, "Well, that explains a whole fucking lot."

Phoenix's eyes widened, Copper snorted, and I just stared at her. She pointed at Phoenix, "You've been acting weird for the last few weeks." Then she turned her attention back to me, "And you look almost identical to my daughter."

"I'm sorry, doll face. I only kept it from you because I was worried about you and the babies," Phoenix said sincerely.

"I know that, big guy. What I don't know is

what you won't let me do," she said, clearly annoyed with having to ask again.

"Donate bone marrow. He was saying he didn't know if the doctor would allow it since you just gave birth," Aim said.

Annabelle's forehead scrunched. "Why would I need to donate bone marrow?"

Aim flicked his gaze to me and nodded subtly before focusing on Annabelle. "Because my daughter is sick, and she's probably going to die if we don't find a donor." He extended his hand to her, "My name is Amos Edwards, and I'm your half brother."

Annabelle shook his hand, but didn't utter a word.

He then turned to me and held out his hand. "Hi, Layla. It's nice to officially meet you. I'm sorry about the way we met before. I was undercover and couldn't tell you," he said quietly.

"Yeah, I know that now. Uh, sorry about having you arrested and almost blowing your case," I said and felt my cheeks flush.

He laughed. "Can't say I wasn't pissed when it happened, but it all worked out in the end."

"Doll face, you okay?" Phoenix asked, and we all turned our eyes to Annabelle.

"I, um," she started but closed her mouth. "I'm sorry. Let's start over. What in the actual fuck is going on?"

"Maybe we should step outside," Aim suggested.

"Don't bother," I snorted. "That one'll follow us, and that one probably will, too," I said and pointed at Phoenix first, then Copper.

So, right there in Copper's hospital room, Aim told us his story, and then I shared mine. When we were finished, Annabelle filled us in on her past. And I could safely say, we had some fucked-up history.

"Where's your daughter?" I asked.

"She's here in the hospital, on the pediatric unit," he glanced at his watch. "I actually need to be getting back to her."

"Can she have visitors?" Annabelle asked.

Aim smiled. "Only family."

Annabelle and I both stood. "Let's go."

"Not so fast, Locks," Copper, who I thought was asleep, rumbled. "Stay with Phoenix."

I rolled my eyes, but agreed. "Sir, yes, sir," I said and kissed his cheek.

I started to turn away to follow Aim and Annabelle, but Copper circled my wrist and held firm. "Don't be a smartass about me worrying about you. I love you, and I damn sure don't want anything to happen to you."

I nodded and closed my eyes for a brief moment. "I'm sorry. You're absolutely right. And I love you, too. I'll stay with Phoenix, and I won't be gone long."

35

COPPER

The moment Phoenix and Aim left with Annabelle and Layla, Bronze and Badger entered my room. Bronze had been at my bedside almost as much as Layla had, but I wasn't expecting to see Badger.

"Looking good, Copper. How're you feeling?" Badger asked as he reached for my hand.

"Been better, but under the circumstances, I can't complain," I said honestly. Yes, my fucking chest hurt even with all the shit they were giving me for pain, but I was alive and my loved ones were safe.

Badger looked toward the door and motioned with his hand for someone to enter, make that two someones. "Copper, this is my Old Lady, Macy. And this little firecracker is Evelyn Carmichael."

I couldn't hide my surprise when my eyes landed on the woman Badger introduced as Evelyn. "She can't be. Layla said she was in her seventies."

Evelyn laughed, "You just might be my new favorite person, boy. Now, where's my sweet Kayla, I mean Layla?"

"She just stepped out, but she shouldn't be gone too long," I told her, then gestured to the chair. "Please, have a seat."

"Thank you. Wouldn't mind standing, but this confounded hip's making a weakling out of me," she grumbled.

"How is your hip? Badger said you fell and broke it a few weeks ago?"

"It's been a pain in the butt, literally. I made it all these years without ever breaking a bone in my body, but it figures when I finally do, I pick one that's a doozy. But that's enough about me. Tell me, how's my girl? I've been so worried about her."

"She's had a rough go of it the past few months, but it looks like things are turning around for her. She's going to be so happy to see you, but be careful with her. She has a couple of fractured ribs she tends to forget about," I told her.

She grinned. "You're telling the old woman with the broken hip to be careful with the young woman with broken ribs?"

"Yes, ma'am," I said honestly.

"I think I just might like you, Copper. Badger tells me—"

A shriek of delight interrupted Evelyn as Layla's eyes landed on her. "Evelyn!!!" she squealed and darted for the woman.

"Broken bones!" I yelled. "Both of you have broken bones."

With that, Layla slowed her approach, but embraced Evelyn in a fierce hug.

"Are you okay?" they both asked at the same time and then laughed.

"Oh, I've been so worried about you, sweetheart, but from what I hear, it sounds like you're doing okay," Evelyn said in a shaky voice.

Layla sniffled and wiped her eyes. "I've been worried about you, too. I was going to come back, but I got lost and then it snowed, and—"

"It's okay, sweetie. Everything worked out like it was supposed to, and you're safe now," Evelyn said and patted her cheek.

"What happened? When you came back that day? Did he hurt you?" Layla asked.

Evelyn glanced around the room and took in her surroundings before she answered. "Maybe we should save this part of the story for another time."

Badger closed the door to the room to give us as much privacy as possible. "Evelyn, you can speak freely in front of Copper. I've known him since he was a little boy, and I can assure you he's trustworthy." When Evelyn's only response was to raise an eyebrow, Badger added, "He's also a Blackwing. The President of the Devil Springs Chapter."

Evelyn grinned and patted Layla's thigh. "Go big or go home, right, Layla? Good for you, dear."

Layla blushed and covered her face with her hands, but Evelyn kept right on talking. "Well, to answer your questions, I came home that day to find Travis in my house bleeding from what used to be his left eye, and you were nowhere to be found. I managed to get rid of him, but I was in a hurry to get out and look for you, and I fell down the front steps and broke my damn hip."

"I'm sorry for—" Layla started.

"Don't you dare apologize for what you did to him. He said enough for me to figure out what really happened. I'm just glad you were able to get away."

"Where is your son now?" I asked. It would kill me to do it, but I would have to send the boys out to get him. I wasn't in any shape to go hunting for the bastard, and I wouldn't be any time soon.

"Well, that's the part of the story I'm thinking might be wise to keep to myself," Evelyn said cryptically.

"And why is that?" I asked. Surely, she wasn't trying to protect her son after what he did to Layla.

"Not for the reason you're over there thinking, sonny boy. I know how you brothers are about speaking in front of the women," she said and cast her gaze to Layla, then Macy.

"Oh, uh, we'll just step out into the hall and give you a few minutes to talk," Macy said and reached for Layla's hand.

I started to protest, but Badger stopped me. "Isaac and Grady are out there. They'll be fine."

When the girls left, Evelyn shared the rest of her story. "I saw a beat-up truck I didn't recognize when I pulled up to the cabin and immediately knew something wasn't right. I got my gun from the glove box and went inside to make sure Kay—Layla was okay. Well, after seeing the house ransacked, I knew who was there and that he was after money. I found him pacing in the living room, high as a kite and blabbering on and on about all kinds of nonsense. So, I told him I had some money hidden in his father's old tool box out in the shed behind the house. I kept the gun pointed at him and told him where to find the key. When he saw that the drawer was empty, he turned around and started for me, so I shot him."

Badger and I both sat in stunned silence for long minutes after she finished speaking. Finally, I managed to ask, "And then what happened?"

She huffed in annoyance. "I left his dead ass there and went back into the house to grab the radio so I could call the Sheriff to help me find Layla. I was in such a confounded hurry that I tripped or slipped on something and fell down the stairs. I probably would've laid there and died if I hadn't had that radio in my hand."

Badger scratched his head. "Are you saying he's still in the shed?"

"I reckon he is, unless an animal smelled him and drug him off somewhere, which is a likely possibility since that shed was barely standing as it was. Wouldn't have been hard for 'em to get in," she explained.

"Did you tell the Sheriff about Travis?" I asked.

She shook her head. "No, I told him a little about Layla, but didn't tell him her name. Guess it wouldn't have mattered since the clever little thing told me a fake one. I said I was rushing out to look for her and fell. He didn't believe me for one second, but the funny thing was, that part was the honest truth."

"I need to make a trip out to my cabin and check on things. I'll stop by yours and make sure everything's as it should be," Badger said.

"Well, don't make a special trip on my account," Evelyn retorted.

"Don't worry about it, Evelyn. I'll make sure everything is taken care of," Badger assured.

Macy and Layla came back into the room, and we spent the next hour talking and catching up. By the time everyone left, I was more than ready to fall asleep. I patted the bed beside me. "You want to take a nap?"

Layla grinned, "Hell, yes. I'm exhausted."

"Yeah, today's been full of excitement. Speaking of, how'd things go upstairs?"

"About as good as they could have I guess. His daughter is precious. She's so sweet and happy, even though she's extremely sick," she said.

"Did you agree to get tested?" I asked.

She held out her arm to show me the cotton ball taped to the inside of her elbow. "Already did. Annabelle can't and neither can Ember, but Coal got tested, and I think some of the other club members did, too."

"Did you get to meet Ember?" I asked.

"No, she's in Croftridge with her husband, but she's not an option because she's pregnant."

"How long will it take to get the results?" I asked.

"Anywhere between one day and one week, though Splint said he was going to talk to someone down in the lab and see if they could put a rush on it. Oh, I did get to see the babies!"

"Do they have names? Everyone keeps calling them the twins or the babies. Hell, I don't think anyone's said if they're boys or girls."

Layla laughed, and it was so good to hear. "They had one boy and one girl. They named the girl Blaze and the boy Flint. Annabelle is supposed to send some pictures to my phone later tonight. They're so cute."

"You want kids?" I asked.

She stiffened for a second before she blew out a breath and answered. "For a while, I didn't think I would ever be in a place in my life that would be a good time to have children, but I've always wanted them," she admitted.

"Good, because I'm planning on knocking you up as soon as I can get out of this hospital," I growled.

"Copper," she scoffed. "Be serious."

"Dead fucking serious, Locks. As soon as I'm back on my feet, we're getting married, and I'm putting a baby in your belly. Maybe you can convince Evelyn to hang around and play grandma."

"You really mean it?" she asked, sounding like she was about to cry.

"Said it. Meant it. Now, close your eyes and go to sleep."

"I love you, Copper Black."

"Love you, too, Locks."

COPPER

By the time I was finally discharged from the hospital, I was more than ready to go. Even Phoenix's premature babies were sent home before I was. I felt like I had a list a mile long of things to do and was itching to get started on it.

To my surprise, everything I thought was on the list had already been taken care of. Badger did find Evelyn's son's body in her shed and decided the best course of action was to burn down the shed. Can't say I blamed him. I don't think I would willingly move a four or five-week-old corpse either.

Evelyn decided to keep her cabin as a rental and moved to a little cottage just down the street from my place. I was a little worried about her being so close, but she stayed busy with her friends from the senior center and had yet to stop by unannounced.

As for the Disciples of Death, they were no longer a club. After Asp was killed and Aim's cover was revealed, the remainder of the club members were arrested. Most were planning to take a plea bargain for a reduced sentence, but even with that, none of them would be out in the next decade—if they survived prison.

With all the loose ends tied up, I was finally able to get back to actual business. We had purchased three new rental properties just before the club was attacked and those properties still needed work before they could be rented.

"Are you ready to go?" Layla asked.

"Yeah, Locks," I said and rose from my seat. I was still sore as hell and moving slower than I would've liked, but I was also happy to be moving.

Layla huffed when I climbed into the driver's seat of my truck. She didn't want me to drive, but I'd been cleared by my doctor—for the truck, not the bike—and damn it, I was driving.

Twenty minutes later, we walked into the hospital and found our friends and family lining the walls of the waiting area. Badger caught my eye and pointed across the hall where I saw Phoenix leaning against the door frame.

We made our way over to the room, and Phoenix stepped aside to let us in. Coal was kicked back in the bed like he didn't have a care in the world while Annabelle and Kathleen fussed over him. "Ladies, save some of this for after the procedure," I said jovially.

"Copper!" Annabelle exclaimed with delight. "You didn't have to come."

"Gee, it's good to see you, too," I joked.

"Oh, shut it. You know what I meant. How are you feeling?"

"Getting better every day. And you're looking good. You doing okay?" I asked. She truly didn't look like she'd just delivered twins a few weeks ago.

Before she could answer, I heard Layla squeal excitedly. "Oh, my goodness gracious! Aren't you two just the cutest little babies ever?" I turned to find her crouched down in front of a double stroller gazing at Blaze and Flint.

"For now," Ember said with a laugh and rubbed her protruding belly.

Annabelle sighed, "Apparently, there's no age limit on sibling rivalry."

I wrapped my arm around Ember's shoulders and pulled her in for a side hug. "All the babies in this family are cute. I mean, just take a look at the adults."

She laughed and then groaned. Dash was by her side immediately. "What's wrong?"

"I need to pee, and that means I have to stand up, and I don't want to," she whined.

"Come on," he said softly as he helped her to her feet.

"Are you sure there's just one in there?" I asked in all seriousness.

"After I've had this kid and you're all healed up, I'm going to kick your ass," Ember said with a mischievous grin on her face as Dash led her from the room.

I chuckled and made my way over to the bed. Clapping Coal on the shoulder, I said, "Proud of you, man."

He shrugged. "Nothing to be proud of. Family is family, and I'm happy to help."

"Knock, knock," a nurse called from the door. "It's time."

Layla and I stepped out into the hall so

Phoenix, Annabelle, Kathleen, Jeff, and Ember could have a moment with Coal before they took him down for the procedure.

"Do you think it will work?" Layla asked quietly.

"I don't know, Locks. But, if it doesn't, maybe enough time will have passed for Annabelle or Ember to be able to donate if they're a match."

She sniffled and wiped under her eyes. "I wish I was a match."

"I wish I was, too," Amos said from behind Layla.

"Hey, big brother. How's Abigail today?" Layla asked.

Amos grimaced and shook his head. "She's had better days."

While Layla and Amos were talking, Phoenix caught my attention and jerked his head in the direction of the hall. I excused myself and left Layla chatting with her siblings.

Phoenix started without preamble. "When Coal transfers to your club, I'm sending Savior with him. It wasn't a request a from him, and it's not a request from me."

"Is there something I need to know about?" I asked, unsure of how to react to his declaration.

Phoenix wouldn't pass a problem off to another chapter; he'd deal with it himself. From what I understood, Savior was a highly regarded brother.

Phoenix shook his head. "No, it's not my story to tell, but the reason behind it has nothing to do with the club. He's dealing with a lot of guilt, and the source of that guilt moved to Devil Springs a few months ago. I think he'll be better if he's closer."

"Is this about a girl?" I asked.

Phoenix snorted. "Technically, yes, but not in any way like you're thinking."

I shrugged. "Doesn't sound like I have much of a choice, but we'd love to have Savior."

Phoenix nodded resolutely. "Yeah, I hate to lose him, and Ranger is going to be supremely pissed, but he's going downhill fast. He needs this."

"Does he know you're sending him to me?" I asked.

"Nope. Wanted to tell you first. Just…keep an eye on him and let me know if he's not doing okay."

"Sure, man. Like I said, we're happy to have him."

"Now, about my wife's sister?" he asked.

"I love her," I answered honestly.

"You gonna marry her?"

I laughed, "Eventually. I already made her my Old Lady."

Phoenix chuckled. "Always trying to be like me."

I couldn't deny that. I loved my older cousin and had always looked up to him. It was an honor to be like him.

ACKNOWLEDGMENTS

Cover Design: C.T. Cover Creations

Cover Model: George RJ

Cover Photographer: James Critchley

Proofreading/Copyediting: Kathleen Martin

Bronze

Coal

Standalones

Beached

Christmas in Tinsel Town

ABOUT THE AUTHOR

Website/Newsletter Sign-up
www.teaganbrooks.com

Reader Group
https://www.facebook.com/groups/tbbooks

Society6 Store
https://society6.com/teaganbrooks

facebook.com/teaganbrooksbooks

twitter.com/teaganbrooks1

instagram.com/teaganbrooksbooks

bookbub.com/profile/teagan-brooks

Made in the USA
Columbia, SC
07 May 2020